"You'll be able to do what no other girl can do."
    She gets my attention with that one.

"You're lucky to have this chance. Girls would kill to take your place."

This is what my mother tells me. She's been chewing her lip for the past three weeks, thinking about my aunt's suggestion to make me into a boy. She seems to have woken this morning with her mind made up. She knows I'm nervous and I can tell she is too. I don't know how people will react to me. I'm not even sure how *I'll* react to me.

"It won't be forever."

Maybe that's where the problem is.

Also by
Nadia Hashimi

The Sky at Our Feet

NADIA
HASHIMI

One
Half
from
the
East

HARPER

An Imprint of HarperCollinsPublishers

Library of Congress Control Number: 2016938972
ISBN 978-0-06-242191-3

Typography by Erin Fitzsimmons
17 18 19 20 21   BVG   10 9 8 7 6 5 4 3 2 1

First paperback edition, 2018

For Kyrus,
who breathes magic into
our lives every day.

where are you from I asked

she smiled in mockery and said

one half from the east

one half from the west

one half made of water and earth

one half made of heart and soul

one half staying at the shores and

one half nesting in a pearl

—From the poem "You Are Drunk,"
by Jalal ad-Din Muhammad Rumi,
thirteenth-century Persian poet

One
Half
from
the
East

One

Sleep, Obayda, and by morning all will be forgotten.

My mother's advice worked quite well for most troubles: an argument with my sister, a bad grade, a tear in my favorite dress. But six months ago, something so bad happened that even her wisdom could not see me through it. As hard as I try, the memory won't go away and that's because a reminder of that gruesome day lives in my home and calls me daughter.

I try to focus on my father's gentle face or his perfectly complete hands, but my eyes always drift down to where his leg used to be and everything comes back in one horrible rush.

On that terrible day at the very beginning of spring,

my father had taken me to see the doctor. My parents were worried because I'd been coughing for two whole weeks and my throat was so sore I could hardly eat. The doctor looked in my throat and put a stethoscope to my chest. When he was done, he gave my dad a prescription for antibiotics. On our way home, my father decided we should stop by the pharmacy to pick up the medication.

I was so tired from all the walking. It was morning and my father still wanted to get to work in the afternoon. He found a plastic chair outside a clothing store and told me to wait for him there. I watched him walk the two blocks down the street and go into the pharmacy. When he came out, he had a small paper bag in his hand. He lifted it into the air and waved at me with a smile. That medicine was for me and it's the only reason we were in the market that day. I try not to think about that too much.

A second later, a white car pulled up in front of the pharmacy and blocked my view. I waited for my father to reappear.

After that, things get pretty fuzzy. I remember the loudest sound I've ever heard. I remember smoke and screaming and people running. I remember horns and fire and the sound of glass breaking. I remember putting my hands over my ears and falling to the ground.

I stayed that way for a long time—waiting for the sounds to stop.

I looked up and tried to find my father, but where I'd last seen him standing there was only the car. It was missing its hood and inside the car was one big ball of flames.

I'm sure I was crying. I don't know if I was screaming. My throat hurt even more the next day, so I probably had been.

Everyone was trying to get away from the white car. Everyone but me.

I ran right into the smoke, which I now know was a bad idea, but I wasn't really thinking straight. There were people on the ground. I looked only at their faces. I ignored everything else.

I grabbed my father from under his arms and tried to drag him away from the car, but he was too heavy. A couple of men helped me—one on either side. They started doing something to my father's leg. I was waiting for my father's eyes to open and didn't pay much attention to anything aside from his face. I just wanted him to talk to me.

It wasn't until we were at the hospital that I realized the men had used their jackets to wrap up the wound where half my father's leg had been blown off. Their brown jackets turned dark and wet in a way that made my stomach lurch.

It was the worst thing I've ever seen, and I'm glad I don't remember more of it.

My father stayed in the hospital for weeks. We didn't visit him much that spring because my mother said it was no place for children.

He came home with a stump wrapped in white gauze, half of his leg gone. He couldn't move around and needed help with everything. We lived on the third floor of our building, which meant that once he got into the apartment, it was really hard for him to leave because there was no elevator. My father was angry and tired all the time, probably because he was in a lot of pain. He was at his worst when his pain medications wore off or when my mother was fixing up his bandages. My mother changed the dressings on his stump every two days. She would wipe the crust off the raw, fleshy part and rewrap it as gently as she could. It was gruesome to look at. I saw it a few times and, after that, I would make up some excuse to leave the room any time she undid the gauze strips.

Eventually the end turned into knobby skin and my father didn't seem to be as angry. Instead, he turned into a ghost. I don't mean that he died, but that he could be in a room and people hardly knew he was there. If he talked, it was in a light whisper. Most of the time he stayed in the bedroom he shared with my mother. When he got a little better, he would come out once every couple of days but avoided all conversation by saying his leg hurt. It gave him a good excuse to be alone and sleep, which is all he wanted to do. I suppose he was trying to forget, too.

Since my father got hurt, he couldn't work as a police officer anymore. I miss seeing my father smile and having him hold my hand when we walk through the market. I didn't realize how proud I was of him until he lost his uniform.

This fall, much more has changed than the color of the leaves. We had to pack up and move to the village to be closer to my father's brothers so they could help us out. And living in an apartment at the top of three flights of stairs wasn't a great idea for a man with one leg.

We moved from Kabul to a village in the middle of nowhere, and that's where we live now, in a dry valley. Most of the red, orange, and gold leaves have turned brown under the feet of villagers. My father grew up here but moved to Kabul, where my mother's family lived, as a young man.

Life in Kabul was so much better. Our apartment had a balcony, which I really liked because I could see everything that was happening in the street or in the balconies below us. I loved leaning over the railing and watching drivers roll down their windows and yell at each other, their cars just inches apart. My school in Kabul was in a really nice building. It was messed up so badly during the war that they had to rebuild a lot of it. We had blackboards and desks and a playground with swings.

The village is far from Kabul and very different. There aren't as many people and there are nowhere near as many cars. Families live closer to each other and there are no apartment buildings. We live in a small home close to my uncles' houses. Our village home has a courtyard, but there's nothing exciting to see there unless you like watching clothes dry on a line. My eldest uncle takes care of his younger siblings plus his own wife and children. That's the way things go. The oldest boy in the family is the one who's responsible for looking after everyone. He's sort of like the backup father.

But my family doesn't have a son, which means we don't have a backup father.

Like our Kabul apartment, our village home has an "everything" room, which is basically our living room but more. Our everything room in Kabul was painted yellow, but the one in our new home doesn't look like it's been painted at all. We moved all that we had in our old everything room into our new everything room.

Here in the village, we have a single television against the wall with a DVD player, which we use to watch pirated movies we bought from street vendors in Kabul. The only problem is, we can't do this very often since electricity is really unreliable. The earth floor is hidden by a few burgundy carpets woven with intricate geometric patterns.

Along the sides of the rooms are long, flat cushions we lie on with big pillows propped against the wall. My mother likes to rest her back on these pillows while she's sewing. When it's dinnertime, we lay a vinyl tablecloth on the ground and eat. On weekends, which are Fridays and Saturdays, we welcome guests here (which means bringing them tea and dried fruits). When it's cold out, we use a low stove with hot coals at the base. We cover the stove with a thick blue-and-gray plaid comforter so we can sit around it and warm ourselves. We set bowls of walnuts nearby and snack on them. In the afternoons, we spread out our notebooks from Kabul and review old homework assignments. My sisters and I read side by side, sometimes helping one another if we get stuck on a word. When my mother is in a good mood, we can get her to play cards with us. We play games called "five card" or, my favorite, "game of the thief." The loser has to do something awful, which usually means washing the dishes.

There are two other rooms—one room for my parents to sleep in and one room that I share with my sisters. We all sleep on thin mattresses that rest on the floor. In the mornings, we fold our blankets and lay them on our beds. There's also a small room that opens to the back of the house, and that's where my mother does the cooking, letting the smell of sautéed onions escape into the open air.

It's a pretty simple house, not made of any concrete or metal like our apartment building in Kabul, but my mother keeps reminding us that things could be worse. I think she just tells us that so we won't keep talking about how much better things used to be.

My mother tries really hard. She's not happy about living in this village. It's far from her family and friends. She misses our home in Kabul. She misses the hair salon she would go to (even if she went only once a year) and the new sofa we'd just bought for our home. I think she misses the way my father used to be too. It's a lot harder to make her laugh now, even when I'm being really funny.

And I know my mother is not all that happy about being closer to my father's family. My aunts come and talk to her, but she either gives them tight, polite smiles or looks like she's trying not to roll her eyes. Everyone lives so close to us it takes only a few minutes to walk from house to house. And it's not like we can pretend we're not home. We're always home because there's nowhere to go.

I can see this stuff now because I'm ten years old and not a child anymore. My father's leg taught me a lot about my parents. I can see they're not always strong and they're not always right.

And because I'm ten years old and smart enough to

notice, I see that lately my mother's been giving me a strange look—like she's got something bad to tell me. But I know she's going to do what parents do and pretend that it's actually something good.

Two

I hear a knock on the outside door, the one that separates our courtyard from the street. I open the door for my father's brother and his wife. This is their third time coming by this week. I don't mind my uncle. He's the oldest in the family and looks it. He's tall with a heavy belly and a round face. He smiles when he sees me or my sisters but doesn't talk to us a whole lot. On the other hand, I don't really like being around his wife, Khala Aziza, but she is my aunt, so I have to be nice. She's the kind of lady who starts every sentence with *Let me tell you what you should do.* That's her thing.

She loves to talk too. We moved to this village almost three weeks ago, in the beginning of fall. My sisters and

I were looking forward to going to school, even though it was nearly the end of the school year, which starts in the spring and lets out for three months in the winter.

During the first week in our new home, Khala Aziza came over every day, until she was sure she had told my mother everything she needed to know about each and every person in our whole extended family.

"Where's your father?" my uncle asks.

"In the bedroom," I tell him. It's the same answer I've given all week. My uncle walks into the house, says a quick hello to my mother, and makes a right. My aunt pulls me toward her and draws my face into her hands.

"How are you, dear? Are you doing well?"

"I'm fine, thanks." I'm thrown off by her asking me. I'm the youngest in the family and don't really have any gossip to share with her. Since she's still holding my face, I try talking my way out of her hands. "Er, how . . . how are you?"

"Surviving, I suppose." It works. She lets go of my face and shakes her head. I try to look around her and see if one of my sisters is nearby. I need a way out of this strange conversation, but there's no one else in the courtyard— just the two of us.

"My mother is inside. Why don't you come in?" I say in my most polite voice.

"I will, I will." But she doesn't move. She's got her hands

on my shoulders now, so I'm trapped.

"Obayda, you're such a bright girl," she says. "I think you could do so much for your family."

I have no idea what she means by this.

"Uh, thanks . . ."

She leans in. I'm so close I could count her eyelashes if I wanted to.

"You can help your father," she whispers. "You can make him proud."

I smile awkwardly and wiggle my shoulders to loosen her grip. I can't wait for Mother to enroll us in school. I'd much rather not be home when my aunt comes by. Mother's promised we'll start soon. She hates for us to miss any school and fall behind in our studies.

"Okay, Auntie, but I have to go . . . Meena is waiting for me," I blurt out and run into the house. I race past my mother.

"Obayda, where are you going?" she calls after me as she pulls herself off the floor cushion.

"Khala Aziza is here," I say without stopping.

I run into the bedroom I share with my sisters: Neela, Meena, and Alia. Neela is sixteen years old, Meena is thirteen, and Alia is twelve. They're all older than me, and I've spent my life either chasing after them or running away from them. That's how it goes for the youngest in the house.

Meena is on her hands and knees, patting the carpet. I flop onto my sleeping cushion and pick up my stuffed panda.

"What are you doing, Meena?"

"I lost my earring," she mutters.

"Again?"

Meena's had these tiny gold hoops since she was a baby. I put the panda down and crawl onto the carpet to help her. The earring has a way of blending into the pattern of the rug.

"Auntie Aziza is here."

"Yeah, I heard her voice."

"She's acting weird," I tell Meena quietly.

"Look over there. I've already checked this part." I scoot over a couple of feet. She's let me wear her earrings a few times, and I love the way the hoops dance on my earlobes. That's why I'm willing to help her look.

"Meena, did you hear what I said? She's saying strange things."

"Like what?"

"Like that I should make our father proud."

"That's not that strange, Obayda." Meena jumps to her feet. "I found it!"

I watch her slip the hoop back into her ear.

"Meena . . ."

Meena shoots me a sly look.

"Come," she says. "Let's go see what Khala Aziza's talking about."

Meena takes my hand and leads me into the short hallway. We tiptoe past the room my parents sleep in. My uncle is sitting with his back to the doorway, talking to my father in a low voice. They don't notice us creeping past them. We stop just outside the living room. Meena puts her finger up to her lips, reminding me to stay silent. My aunt is not afraid that someone may be listening. We hear every word.

"We all see it. He won't talk, not even to his brother. He won't get out of bed. He's barely eating. How is he supposed to get any better if you don't do something?"

"I think he just needs some time . . ."

"He's had lots of time, my dear. If you care about his health, you'll do the right thing."

"I just can't do that to Obayda. It's not right. I don't want to change her. She's such a . . . a girl. She loves her dresses and her dancing and her sisters. I don't want to take all that away from her."

My shoulders tense when I hear my name. Meena's looking at me with her eyebrows raised.

"She'll learn to love new things. And she can always go back to loving those things in a few years. It's the perfect solution. It's a simple change and doesn't cost you any more than a couple of pairs of pants."

"He loves his daughters. He always has. But I do remember when he used to talk about wanting a son."

"That's exactly what I'm saying! You know what a difference it would make for him. You've seen my husband talk about our three sons, haven't you? Oh, his face just glows when he gets started on them. A son can do for your husband what no doctor can."

"You really think so? And wouldn't it be hard on her? I mean, she's a girl. I can't just make her wake up as a boy."

"It's much easier than you think. And Obayda will love it. When I was a young girl, my neighbor was a *bacha posh*. She was my age, and we used to play together until her mother changed her into a boy. Then she ran with the boys and was too busy to have anything to do with me. She was the happiest girl in our neighborhood, I promise. Do it now, before the girls start school. It'll be easier on everyone."

My eyes go wide. Is she suggesting what I think she's suggesting?

"And for how long do we keep her that way?" My mother sounds unsure.

"It's very simple, dear. Make Obayda into a boy. With her as a son, she will bring good luck to your home. You'll see your husband cheer up. Then you plan for another baby in the family. Having a *bacha posh* at home brings boy energy into your household. The next baby that comes will be a boy. And once you have a real son, watch what happens. Your husband will come back to life. I've seen this work in the families around us. It's not magic—it's just how it is. And that's when Obayda can go back to being a girl. Everyone wins."

I hear my mother sigh.

"How will I make her believe it? How will I make her sisters believe it?"

"Make her not just a son, but the most precious son that ever lived. Take away her chores. Don't let her do anything that girls usually do. Tell her she's a boy with every bite of food you feed her, with every word you speak to her, with every pass you give her on her boyish trouble-making."

My mother is silent. She must be thinking this over.

"And there's something else you'll need to think about," my aunt warns. "You must know that the brothers cannot go on supporting an entire family forever. A boy can work and earn money. A boy is good luck. A boy brings other boys into the family. Girls can't do any of those things. You're not in Kabul anymore, my dear. This town is run by that awful warlord Abdul Khaliq, and if you don't throw yourself at his feet, it's hard to scrape by. Time to think seriously about what you can do for your family. You don't want to see your daughters go hungry, do you?"

"Of course not," my mother whispers. It sounds like her voice is cracking.

Meena takes my hand into hers and squeezes. There is a pause. I can hear my aunt pouring herself a cup of tea.

"Make Obayda your son, and let him fix everything that's wrong with your family."

Three

"You'll be able to do what no other girl can do."

She gets my attention with that one.

"You're lucky to have this chance. Girls would kill to take your place."

This is what my mother tells me. She's been chewing her lip for the past three weeks, thinking about my aunt's suggestion to make me into a boy. She seems to have woken this morning with her mind made up. She knows I'm nervous and I can tell she is too. I don't know how people will react to me. I'm not even sure how *I'll* react to me.

"It won't be forever."

Maybe that's where the problem is.

My mother wields a pair of scissors, blades that usually nip pieces of string or folds of paper or stems of mint—nothing as important as this. She looks unsure.

So am I.

For ten years I've been a girl. That's a pretty long time. I like being a girl. I like doing girl things. My mother tells me that as a baby, I danced before I walked. I would crawl up to a table, pull myself to stand, and sway side to side to the rhythm of the music on my father's radio. I love when the song starts slow and then moves into tabla-drum rumbles, fingers beating against an animal skin stretched taut, and the song goes wild. It's fast and exciting, and I can't help but bounce to it.

By the time I was four, I had memorized a few dances from some Indian movies. I'd put on my fullest skirt and sneak one of my mother's head scarves from her dresser. My favorite was the purple-and-gold one my sisters had outgrown. With the ends of the scarf in my outstretched fingertips, I would pivot on one foot, my right shoulder dipping in and flaring back, in and back, in and back.

Neela, Meena, and Alia love to watch me dance, though they can't keep from telling me what I'm doing wrong.

"Don't forget your eyes!" my sisters would chide. "The eyes are so important. They tell the story of the song."

Meena heard an Indian movie star say so once in an interview. I would keep mine wide, my eyeballs rolling from corner to corner and my lips curled in a coy smile. I learned how to flip my head just right so all my hair would fall to the side.

I couldn't mess up a single move. My sisters would call me on it if I did.

My wrists would twirl together in a wide arc over my head. I loved when my sisters would clap for me.

When I was around six years old and Alia was eight, she decided we should re-create the duet dance, one where a man and woman flirt with each other. The woman in the movie pretends not to be interested, but the guy chases after her because he loves her so much. I was given the part of the guy because Neela and Meena thought I'd be better at it. It wasn't as much fun at first. I missed making my skirt billow out as I twirled, looking like a spinning top. But I could do it. Shoulders back, hips forward, head cocked to the side. Alia's steps were delicate and graceful like the song of a flute; mine were heavy and bold like fists thumping on a drum.

Leaning in, I would take playful steps toward my sister, grabbing the end of her head scarf just as the actor did in the movie. Hand over hand, I'd pull her closer to me, in a tug-of-war that no woman ever won. I was the victor, the conqueror, the man.

But that was pretend, and what my mother is talking about now is very different. She's talking about a real change, not something I'll stop doing at the end of a song.

"You won't have to worry about tying your hair back. Remember last Friday, when you wanted to hang upside down from the branch of that old poplar tree in the park? How long have you been asking me to let you run with the boys when they chase each other through the streets? How many times have you asked to ride your cousin's bicycle? Today is the day I will tell you yes. *Yes, yes, yes.*"

My mother is good. If she were one of those kids who sold sticks of stale gum on the street, all the foreigners would buy from her.

My sisters follow as my mother leads me to the patio behind our four-room house. It's a simple house with nothing on the walls but a prayer in calligraphy and a picture of our family. Our home is surrounded by a courtyard, which sounds fancy but just means there's open space. There's a pear tree in the front and a dried-out acacia tree in the back, where our laundry hangs on a clothesline. The courtyard is closed in with a clay wall that goes all the way around, making our house a box inside a box. There's a gate in the wall that opens into the street where all anyone can see is walls because all homes are made the way ours is. That's what gives us all privacy and keeps neighbors from seeing into our home and us from seeing into theirs.

"Sit on this," she says, pointing to a wooden crate.

"Why don't you do this for them too?" I ask the questions my sisters won't ask. That might be my thing. I've been wondering if I have a thing. It's easier to spot other people's things than it is to pick out my own.

"You're only ten years old. They're too old for this. A boy can't have breasts."

I think about this. Because my sisters are older, their bodies are made of curves and circles. Mine is different. My shoulders and hips are as square as a piece of paper. Neela's definitely got breasts, but Meena's got nothing more than two small lumps that you can't see because she's wearing one of Neela's dresses—one she hasn't quite grown into yet. Alia is too pretty to be a boy. I don't even argue with my mother about her.

I'm raw clay and they're pottery.

"Then why didn't you do it before? Neela was my age six years ago."

"We were in Kabul. Your father was working and we were . . . we were just different then."

I know Kabul was different. In Kabul every family sent their girls to school. In the village, there are two kinds of families. There are the ones that send their daughters to school—and then there are the ones that don't. Some families think daughters are born to be wives and mothers and don't need to bother with books or writing. I feel bad for these girls because they don't get to do all the things schoolgirls do. They can count only how many cups of rice to soak and can't tell the letter *kof* from the letter *gof*. Other families are more like ours and think girls should be able to write their names, read books, and multiply. They still think girls will grow up to be married, but, like my mom always says, a smart girl will be a smarter mother.

I remember what Khala Aziza said about this making my father better. She doesn't seem like the most reliable authority, but if there's even a chance she's right, I should do it. I owe Padar-*jan* that much.

"How long will it take for my hair to grow back?"

My mother doesn't answer.

"Mother, are you sure this is a good idea?"

"Obayda, why wouldn't I be sure?"

She's got a hand on her hip, but she answers my question with a question, which is a sure sign that she doesn't know what the answer is. I wish she would just say that.

My hair falls just past my shoulder blades now. My mother is stroking it, trying to even it out, bracing herself as she prepares to make the first cut. She takes her time. I wonder if she's changing her mind.

I like my long hair. I like having my mother brush it out and braid it—one thick, brave plait. When I turn my head it swings like a horse tail. I like my dresses. I don't tell my sisters, but I like that they've worn them before me because it means I know what I will look like even before I put them on. Alia and I are close enough that we share some of our clothes. That won't happen anymore. Alia can't wear pants.

My mother cuts. The scissors are dull and my hair is thick. It puts up a noble fight.

"You see how easy this is? Now I just need to make it even."

My mother manages to get rid of the length, but she doesn't quite know how to make it look like a boy's head. She just keeps cutting from the ends until I have a shaggy cap of hair. I still look like a girl. My mother takes a step back to judge her work. She looks like she might cry.

Meena steps in and takes the scissors from my mother's hands.

Snip, snip, snip. Clumps of hair fall at my feet.

Some people can look at something and know how to make it better. That's Meena's thing.

When Meena is done, I stand and check out my reflection in the window that looks into our kitchen. My ears are much bigger than I ever realized. I turn my head to the side. There's no horse tail to swing. There are no knots for my mother to gently brush out. My purple hair clips—the plastic ones that look like tiny bows—I can't use at all. My hands are on my head, pulling at nothing. What has she done to me?

"Meena, take her inside so she can change into the

shirt and pants. I'm going to clean up here."

My mother grabs a short broom and starts to sweep my hair from the courtyard.

"I don't need Meena's help. I can dress myself." The words come out with more spunk than I mean them to. I wonder if something's happening to me already.

I go inside and find the blue plastic bag. Inside are a pair of navy blue cargo pants with four pockets, which are four more than I'm used to having, and a gray button-down shirt with a wolf patch sewn onto the left arm, just below my shoulder. The wolf looks fierce, his mouth open just enough to reveal two dramatic fangs. I try to copy his snarl. I put the pants on and feel like I've stepped into another world. Meena comes into the room and stares at my backside.

"I can see your whole body," she whispers.

I'm covered from head to toe, but not with the shapeless shift of a dress. These clothes outline my form so clearly that Meena could (but doesn't) measure the distance from my shoulder to my hip or from my collarbone to my knee. I look over my own shoulder, twisting my neck as far as it will go. I want to see my behind. I want to know what it looks like in pants. It's hard not to feel naked. Aside from when I'm taking a bath or the day I was born, this is as naked as I've ever been.

"Why are you watching me, Meena? Girls shouldn't be

watching boys." It's not something I actually mean. The words and the boldness are things I need to try on—like the cargo pants.

"Oh, that's just great. Now we have to deal with your attitude, too. Don't think I'm going to treat you any differently. You're still Obayda to me, today and tomorrow and all the days after that."

I step in front of her, close enough that she can see the flyaway hairs she missed cutting. "What do you really think? Do I look like a boy? Am I really going to be able to do all those things Madar talked about?"

Meena shrugs. "Why not? You look like you're one of the boys now."

I run my hands over my head. There's nothing to braid, brush, or tangle.

I'm not sure how I feel about this.

"But how will I know for sure that I can do all those things?"

Meena thinks for a second, tapping her finger on her rose lips. "Think of the things that only a boy could do and then go and do them. If everything goes well, then you'll know for sure."

She might be right. In a stroke of brilliance, I come up with a plan to test this out.

I don't have a brother, but I've seen how boys pee. I saw a little boy in the market once, standing by the edge of a ditch. His mother was trying to fan out her skirt and cover him from view, but I could still see. He couldn't have been more than five or six years old, so it was okay for me steal a curious peek. I saw him lean his shoulders back and thrust his hips forward, and a yellow stream made a high arc before landing in the ditch.

I had a plastic gun once. A little orange squirter that I filled with water. If I squeezed it just right, I managed to hit my sister right in the ear, so I think my aim must be pretty good.

I walk into our outhouse, which is a small shack behind our home.

If I can do this, I'll know I can be a boy.

Our outhouse is like any other outhouse. It's got just enough room for one person to stand. There's a hole in the middle with one brick on either side. Usually I crouch down with a foot on each brick and my pee can't help but go into the hole right under me. Easy enough.

I stand with my back to the door. There's just enough light filtering in through the small window on the wall to my right. I pull my new pants down and thrust my hips out, the way the little boy did. I try to peek down and see if this is going to work. Since it's hard to see anything, I point my hips out a little farther. I hope I don't overshoot the hole. My aim with the orange squirter was pretty good, but this is a little different.

I will do this. If I have to be a *bacha posh*, I will be the best *bacha posh* there ever was. My mother will think she's had a son all along.

I let go and a hot stream runs down my leg, soils my new four-pocketed cargo pants, and puddles in my sandals.

Four

"I want to wait a couple of weeks before you start school. A lot has changed for you," my mother tells me. "There are some things you need to get used to since you're a boy now."

My face goes red. I have a feeling she somehow found out about my outhouse experiment yesterday. My mother's not sure what else I might try.

There *are* big things for me to get used to. My name is the biggest. (I'm Obayd now—good-bye, Obayda.) I wake up in the morning thinking my hair is still there, but it isn't. I look at the closet I share with my sisters and see a short stack of clothes I don't recognize. The dresses are off-limits, even my favorite ones. My first day at home as a boy is especially difficult since my sisters aren't around. They started school today, but my mother wants to give me a little more time to settle into my new identity. It's the middle of fall, and I know soon enough winter will be here, along with the three-month winter break. I wonder if she'll let me go to school before then.

"Madar?"

"Yes, sweetheart."

"Cutting my hair and calling me Obayd . . . How is that going to bring us a brother?"

"I don't know how it does, but it does. That's what everyone says."

Everyone is actually one person—my uncle's wife.

"Like some kind of magic?"

"Something like that." She folds my sisters' dresses. Sleeve, sleeve, skirt. The final stack is bulky and looks like it will topple off the pile of clothes she's made next to her.

It is my turn to pause. If my dressing as a boy is an act of magic, shouldn't I feel something? Maybe a tingle in my toes or a whisper in my ear or something to make my senses light with the special role I've been assigned in my parents' scheme? I give it a second, holding my breath. Nope, nothing.

"People say if you dress a daughter like a son, God will give you a son."

"You said I'd be able to do things other girls can't do

and that it would be great for me. But this isn't for me at all."

"It's for all of us. There's nothing we do for any single person here. That's what being a family is. We help each other in whatever way we can."

I do want to be helpful.

"Do you want me to bring the clothes in from outside, Mother?"

My mother nods and points at the basket in the corner of the living room before she catches herself.

"Wait, stop! No, my son. I'll bring them in later."

"But they're already dry. I can fold them and—"

She shakes her head.

"Obayd, just leave them alone and go play in the court-yard."

I shrug my shoulders. It's odd for my mother not to want my help with the housework, but I let it go and head into the courtyard. Alia has left two of her old rag dolls by my father's chili pepper plants—the plants my mother now has to care for. Alia doesn't play with the dolls, but she also can't bear to give them away. I haven't played with dolls in years either. They're also off-limits now that I'm a boy, and that shouldn't bother me, but it does. The dolls are the size of my hand, with dresses as worn as Alia's. Their faces have been painted on with black ink, and I feel like their wide eyes are staring at me. I turn my back to them.

It's my second day as a *bacha posh*, and it's setting out to be a lonely one. My sisters have all gone to school and my mother won't let me help her with the housework. My father wants to be alone, since that's his thing now. I'm left to figure out how to be a boy.

Music starts to stream over the courtyard wall. Our neighbor is playing the radio loudly. The sounds of the drumbeats, the keyboard, and the strumming of a *rubab* carry into our yard. I tap my foot to the rhythm and think about what else I might be able to do.

Boys my age, when not in school, would be out in the street. I've seen them play pickup games of soccer or catch. What would I say? Would they spot me as the girl from down the road? I don't think I can walk out there and join them. I stand up. Maybe being on my feet will help me think.

I could ask for a bicycle. Girls aren't really supposed to ride bicycles, but a boy could. And I'm a boy. I wonder if I could keep it upright like the boys do or if I would topple over.

"Obayd!" my mother yells.

I'm brought back by her sharp tone. I spin around to face her; a basket of dry clothes rests on her hip.

"Yes, Mother?" The look on her face tells me I've done something. "What is it?"

"What is it? I haven't asked much of you, Obayd. I am

only asking you not to do things that a boy shouldn't be doing. Do you know any boy who would dance around like that?"

I hadn't even realized. I look at my feet and it occurs to me that I was swinging my hips to the tempo of the song as I crossed the courtyard. Come to think of it, I'm pretty sure I was bopping my shoulders too. The music just takes me sometimes.

My mother makes a pot of stew with steaming white rice. We sit around the tablecloth spread on the living room floor. Neela asks my father to join us. We all hear him say what he says every day.

"Maybe tomorrow, sweet girl."

My mother piles hot mounds of rice on plates for each of us. Then she stirs the pot of stew with a metal ladle. She pours the saucy mix of chicken and vegetables onto my plate first and then onto my sisters' plates.

"Mother!" Neela cries out in protest when she looks at her dish. "I just have potatoes and onions. I thought you said you made chicken for dinner tonight?"

This is a big deal because it's not too often that we get to eat chicken. My uncle sent some over because of the three-day Eid holiday that marks Abraham's willingness to sacrifice his son for God. I've heard the story before and was really glad to hear God didn't actually take his son. Now it's just a holiday where we pray, visit family, and get to eat really well. We've been looking forward to this meal all day.

"Neela," my mother explains in a low voice. "There wasn't much meat to cook. Your father is still healing and needs the nutrition more than any of us."

My sisters all stare at the plate in front of me. Their eyes narrow in accusation.

"But Obayda—I mean, Obayd's got two big pieces of chicken right there. Even a drumstick!"

I do have more than my fair share. There's nothing left in the pot but sauce and a few chunks of uninteresting vegetables.

"I can give you some of my—"

"No, you will not." My mother keeps her head down and tears off a piece of bread. She's about to take a bite when she pauses and decides to set some ground rules.

"Obayd is a boy. He needs the meat if he's going to get stronger. I don't want to hear any more about it."

Her tone shuts down the conversation. We eat in silence, Neela's jaw clamping down angrily on her dinner. I know she's got no real reason to be angry with me, but I'm pretty sure she is.

My mother calls me into the kitchen. She reaches into the pocket of her dress and slips me a few afghanis, more money than I've ever had in my hands.

"Take this dough to the baker and come back with bread."

It sounds simple enough. I've been to the market plenty of times with my mother. I used to go to the market in Kabul with my father, too, but that was when he had two legs. I walk slowly, watching the people around me to see if anyone notices that I'm in pants for the first time ever. No one seems to realize.

I'm carrying a metal tray with five mounds of dough. I know where the baker is. Stores run down the length of the dirt road that is our main market. The baker's shop is the fifth one on the block of shops, which are really clay-walled cubbies, some bigger than others. Most have carpets covering an earth floor. One is full of beans, flour, spices, and oil. Another contains fabric and a few sets of children's clothes. They don't have doors, though two of them have curtains drawn to the side so the shopkeeper can watch the passersby in the street.

The baker is the busiest of them all. His store is easy to spot even from a distance because it has a red awning over the entrance. The store is a square space big enough for only him and his helper. They have trays of dough on the floor between them, right next to the big open mouth of the oven, a deep clay pot buried in the ground. The baker stares at me with one eye narrowed.

I don't know what to say.

"Which is the dough and which is the boy?" he asks his friend, with a laugh. "Hard to tell when neither one is talking."

I clear my throat. He called me a boy.

"Can you bake these for us?" I hold my arms out a few inches, but I'm still too far for the baker to reach.

"Are your feet stuck? Bring the dough over to me!"

I move because he's loud and abrupt. My arms thrust the tray in front of his face. He shakes his head and takes it. His friend is chuckling when their eyes meet. My face is hotter than the oven. I turn to the side so they can see only a sliver of me. I can't face them, and turning my back to them feels so much worse. I'm not used to being alone around men I don't know.

The roar of an engine makes me turn around. Two black jeeps with tinted windows drive by. I stare at them until I feel a whack on the back of my shoulder. I spin around, not sure what just happened.

"Don't stare," says the baker's helper.

"I wasn't staring," I reply. He's right, though. Cars like the ones that just passed by are not even common in Kabul, where there are way more vehicles than here. Naturally, they caught my attention.

"You'll regret it. Those are Abdul Khaliq's cars, and you don't want to be caught gawking at them."

"Abdul Khaliq— isn't he a warlord?" I remember Khala Aziza mentioning his name.

The baker laughs.

"Well, his twenty bodyguards seem to think so." His voice grows a bit serious. "Just stay out of his way, kid. There's nothing else to know."

He stretches the dough out and lowers it into the oven. Just a few minutes later, he brings it out on a paddle. I can feel their eyes on me. I kick at the ground with my feet and wonder what a real boy would do in my place.

"Take it." The five lumps have been transformed into piping-hot flatbreads, each longer than my arm. I stack them on the tray and hand him the money. I breathe a sigh of relief that my mission was a success.

My mother is waiting at the door when I come home. She exhales deeply and cups my face in her hands.

"I think you're ready to go to school," she declares. It's not just bread I've brought back from the market—it's a sign that I can play the part of a boy in the real world.

Five

"**O**bayd! Obayd!"

My sisters think it's funny to call me by my boy name. If I answer, they laugh, and if I don't, they raise their eyebrows and threaten to tell Madar.

"Cut it out," I bite back. My stomach is churning. I'm finally starting school. My sisters started a couple of weeks ago and have had a lot of catching up to do, since the school year begins in spring and we're starting in the fall. I've watched them pack their notebooks and pencils and head out of the house while I've been home getting used to being a girl-boy so I won't be so awkward about it when I join my classmates, who are already thinking about the winter break that starts in a few weeks. This just means that everyone in my class will be staring at me even harder since I'm new to this school and starting even later than my sisters.

"As you wish, Obayd-*jan*!" Alia says as if she's curtsying before a king. She's dramatic. That's her thing.

At the end of the main road, Neela stops and gives me a hug. She heads down a smaller road to the left to make her way to the girls' high school. It's much narrower than the one in Kabul, but Neela is happy to be out of the house and with girls her age.

I'm glad and not glad when we reach our school.

"It looks so different from our school in Kabul, doesn't it?"

Sometimes Alia can read my mind.

"It looks so old!"

"It's not that old, but it took a beating during the war. My teacher told me they've fixed it up a lot. It was worse before," Meena says, shaking her head.

My sisters adjust their head scarves, making sure the knots are perfectly centered under their chins.

"I liked our school in Kabul," I say. "And I was supposed to move into the third-grade girls' class there. Now we're here and I'm going into the boys' class. I don't know if I'm going to know what to do."

"A classroom is a classroom wherever it is—which is why we should go in. The teachers here are just as strict as the Kabul teachers about being on time. We'll meet here when they let us out. Don't be late," Meena warns. Her voice softens when she sees the look on my face. "And Obayd . . . you'll be fine, okay?"

I blink quickly so my tears won't get very far.

We go into our different classes, since boys and girls are separated. My sisters go to the left and I go to the right, where I find my classroom. There's a woman standing at the door. She's tall and thin and watches me closely as I try to slip in unnoticed. I keep my head down and hope she won't spy my big ears and the body hidden inside these pants.

She stops me with a hand on my shoulder.

"It's your first day, isn't it?"

"Yes, teacher." I stare at my feet. My face is hot.

"Your name?"

I take a deep breath.

"Obayd."

"Obayd," she repeats and tilts my head up with a finger under my chin. "You are Obayd?"

I nod slowly. Other boys file in, walking around me to get to their places on the carpets that are laid out on the ground. It feels like we stand there for about an hour, her staring at my face and me refusing to meet her eyes.

"Obayd," she says once more.

"Yes."

She lets out a breath so big her whole chest moves with it. She knows what I am. She points into the classroom.

"Find a place to sit. You've missed too much already. You have lots of catching up to do if you want to get a decent grade this year."

There are two windows that look out on the schoolyard. I find a place in the third row of students and sit next to the wall.

I take out a notebook and pencil and keep my head down as if I'm about to write something. There are boys all around me, but I don't want to talk to them. I know they'll see right through me and be even worse than my sisters.

The hours are long. We study math, religion, and reading. My teacher, Seema-*jan*, makes us recite verses from our holy book, the Qur'an, which is the toughest subject for me. Reading is a little easier. Most of what we're doing is stuff I learned last year in my school in Kabul. I fidget a lot. The boy next to me notices. He leans in and whispers: "Stop moving around. You're going to get in trouble."

Sitting still was never this hard.

I loved school in Kabul. In the summer, the classrooms were so hot I could barely breathe, but I never complained. We had smooth desks and real chairs. There were blackboards as big as the wall. I had friends who looked like me and a teacher who called me by my real name.

And we knew that we were lucky to be able to go to school at all. Some kids have to work instead. I've seen kids collecting scrap metal from dumps or swinging hammers onto red hot pieces of metal in a blacksmith's shop. Some kids wash cars, shine shoes, or sell pens and sticks of gum. A lot of kids who aren't in school don't get to be kids at all. That made us all really eager to go to class, even if our teachers were strict or assigned lots of hard homework.

We are finally released into the school's playground, which is really nothing more than a big open space with one soccer ball in desperate need of air and a baseball bat that must have been a gift from an American soldier because we don't play baseball in Afghanistan.

Boys play with boys, and girls play with girls. That's always been fine by me. It's not so much that girls and boys want to do different things, but more that we do things in different ways. The girls run a bit on the playground, but without shoving one another or poking fun. The boys are louder and run like they're not afraid of what they might crash into. Their arms swing out and legs stretch forward, crossing as much ground as they can in each bound.

I stare at the girls out of the corner of my eye. I hear them chanting and hopping to the song about pomegranate seeds, the stones in the river, and taking bread to the baker. The words echo in my head as I fight back the urge to join my voice with theirs. My sisters are not in the yard. Their classes will be out later, and I know Meena and Alia will be part of the circles of girls, blending in perfectly.

I watch the boys drift one way and the girls another. I am now in the weird place between both worlds.

I pick up a stick and start walking, hoping no one notices the boy in blue corduroys—the one who is all alone. Three boys are chasing one another. As the first boy flies past me, his sneakers kick up puffs of dust. I take a quick step back so I won't be plowed over by the others. They're on his heels.

"Come, catch him!"

Without slowing their stride, they call out for me to join them.

One boy pauses. He turns around and stares at me. My stomach drops. His face is mostly hidden by the rim of a navy blue American-style cap with W-I-Z-A-R-D-S embroidered across the front in red thread. He is looking at me hard, like I've taken something of his.

"Hey, you! Where are you going?"

I turn to walk in a different direction but he is approaching. I pick up my pace and move closer to the school building.

"Stop!"

I make a quick left and dart into the building, dashing

into the hallway and ducking behind a column wide enough to hide me. I'm panting, and my breaths are loud in the quiet of the empty school. I wait to hear the sound of the door opening, to hear the boy's footsteps in the hallway and for him to find me.

Today he doesn't, but tomorrow—a nervous girl's voice in my head warns me—he will.

Six

By the following day, I am all nerves. I've been a boy for less than three weeks and still haven't fully gotten used to it.

"Obayd. O-BAYD!"

I haven't heard the teacher. My eyes have been on the window, staring at the playground, where I know we'll be heading in just a few moments. I don't know exactly what's going to happen today, but I am certain that boy will be looking for me. Thankfully, he's not in my class.

"Yes, *Moallim-sahib*," I say, startled. That's how we address our teachers, by calling them *esteemed teacher*, since it's not proper to use their real names.

"If you're not going to pay attention, do you see any

purpose in sitting in my classroom?" I hang my head, knowing a classroom full of eyeballs are on me.

"Forgive me, *Moallim-sahib*."

"Can you give the answer to the problem?"

I cannot. She has both hands on her hips, her mouth turned in a deep frown.

"You will have an additional homework assignment today, and tomorrow you will stand before the class and answer the questions I ask of you. I'm sure you'll have an easier time hearing me when you stand up here."

"Yes, teacher," I mumble.

When it's time for recess my stomach churns.

In a burst, we're outside and the boys line up for a game of *ghursai*. *Ghursai* is a tricky game that girls don't ever play but boys love. I've watched the boys in my neighborhood play lots of times and know the rules. The game involves two teams. Each team has a leader, a king who needs to be protected from opponents. The goal is to get the king from one side of the field to the target on the other side. Along the way, everyone is trying to knock over their challengers. Anyone who falls is instantly out of the game.

If that were it, the game wouldn't be so bad. But here's the catch: In *ghursai*, players have to reach their right hands behind their backs and grab their left feet in a tight grip. That makes for a field of hopping, one-armed bandits trying to keep their balance, defend their king from attackers, and get to the other side. And if an opponent unlocks a player's finger-foot grasp, that unlucky player is out of the game.

"What's wrong with you? Come and play."

The boy from yesterday watches to see what I will do. He is wearing pantaloons with a khaki tunic and the same cap he had on yesterday. I know I will attract more attention if I try to hide behind the boys playing marbles, so I nod, as cool as I can, and wander over to join the second huddle, the one with fewer people. The boy is on the other team. He gives a half smirk.

"Hey, giiiiiirls," the tallest boy on my team calls out. I look over in a panic only to realize he is talking to our challengers. "Hey, girls, have you chosen your king yet? The sooner we start, the sooner we can knock you over, so hurry up!"

There are chuckles.

"Are you any good?" asks the boy standing next to me.

I start to shrug my shoulders, but it turns into shaking my head. *Ghursai* is one of those boy things that I know about, but if I try to do it . . . well, I remember what it feels like to have a warm puddle of urine in my shoe.

"I don't know," I mumble. We stand together to listen for Basir's orders. Since he's the tallest boy in the older class, he's the captain. I stare down at our sandals, a collage of leather, rubber, and plastic. None look new, so mine, hand-me-downs from my cousin, blend right in.

"Reeeeeaddy?" the boys call out to us. They're in a loose cluster on the other end of the schoolyard. My heart pounds.

"Boys, grab your feet," Basir commands. "Here we go!"

I lock fingers with toes, my shoulder tight as I reach behind me. I wobble and look around to see if anyone notices. They all look steady on their feet, as if there are magic rods running down their spines that keep their bodies upright.

"Attaaaack!" The battle cry rings out, carrying across the yard and overpowering the sounds of the girls.

"Get him!"

"Watch out—on your left!"

I hop to my right, my left arm flailing, and wishing for a solid chunk of air to steady myself. Basir is just a few feet away.

How are they doing this?

If I can keep a good distance from Basir, I may be able to stay out of the action. That's the strategy I'm going with. I tighten my grip and dig my fingers into the front of my sandal.

I take a few hops forward, a zigzag from where I started. They are on us now. Ten boys taking small hops toward us, shoulders and elbows jutting out as they near my team. The clash begins and boys start bouncing off one another.

"Get him!"

I watch Basir take a few steps forward. Two boys from the other side have been knocked out, falling onto their backsides. I watch them rise and walk over to the sidelines, faces sour.

I direct my attention forward again, reminding myself not to pivot. That's when the boy with the *W-I-Z-A-R-D-S* hat catches my eye. He's staring directly at me, as if there's no one else in the yard.

I bounce in the direction of my teammates, unsettled by his glare.

But he comes straight at me, ignoring the tangle of boys. He rounds his way to me just as I try to bury myself amid my team. I'm not quick enough.

"Look out!"

He's a few inches taller than me, and his eyes are narrowed. His hair is shaggy and uneven. He drives his shoulder into my side, charging at me with a loud grunt. I gasp, my hand slipping from my foot before he even makes contact with my body. I fall to the ground, hands outstretched.

"Got you!" he calls out triumphantly.

"You dog!" I scream. I am angry and frustrated and my hands burn from hitting the earth.

He laughs then turns his attention to the rest of my team, who have, by now, made it halfway across the yard and are completely unaware that I've been knocked out. His friends cheer him on as he knocks out two more boys. I am too frustrated to move. Why has my mother sent me out into the world like this? I don't have what it takes. How could she not see that?

It is easy to dance like a boy. Boys sway side to side and raise their arms like they're hoisting a trophy. That's all they have to do. But everything else about being a boy is hard because it's so different from being a girl. Trying to act like a boy is like learning a whole new language, and I am really struggling to find the words. If I start to cry, there will be absolutely no hope for me.

I'm brought out of my self-pity abruptly. The boys are shouting. My team has been toppled, every last one of them, even Basir. The *W-I-Z-A-R-D-S* boy, who knocked me over, has ripped through my classmates like a vengeful tornado. He will look my way. I should stand.

I can't get to my feet fast enough. I am a tangle of clumsy joints and wimpy muscles. Why did I ever think I could do this? I watch the boy. He is grinning triumphantly. His friend throws an arm around his neck in a playful headlock.

The boy in the gray pantaloons takes off his *W-I-Z-A-R-D-S* cap. He steals a look over his shoulder and stares directly at me. His eyes are sharp, and his hair catches the sun's light. His lips tighten at the disappointing sight of me.

I am still on the ground.

Seven

I carefully tear the last page from my composition notebook and write the letters out.

W-I-Z-A-R-D-S.

I try to say the word. *Why-zar-dis.* What could it possibly mean? I take the slip of paper and bring it to my sister Neela. She is sweeping the living room.

"Neela, can you read this word?"

She looks grateful for an excuse to prop the broom against the wall.

"Which word?" She takes the paper from my hand and stares at it long and hard. I think her eyes might scorch a hole through the letters. "Where did you see it?"

Neela knows a bit more English than I do because she's

gone to school longer and has had more English classes. She's almost finished with high school. I can tell from the look on her face that she's not all that sure what the word means.

"If you don't know, don't make something up," I warn.

"I wasn't going to," she says, but her eyelids are blinking up a storm, so I know she's not being completely honest. "I can't remember what it means. I can ask my English teacher. Where did you see it?"

"Nowhere," I say, turning my face. I may not blink my eyes, but I'm pretty sure I have some other tic that will give me away. "I mean, I can't remember where I saw it. I was just wondering."

"You're acting weird," my sister tells me.

"Not as weird as you," I shoot back. Neela huffs and turns her back to me. I walk away quickly, trying to get away from the words she's just said. I am acting strangely, but I don't want to tell my sister that I'm scared of a boy at school. I don't want her to know that after years of shooting my mouth off at home and playing the part of the heroic film star, I am uncomfortable with my new life in pants and I'm afraid that a boy at school is out to get me. I don't want to sound that pathetic, so I keep it to myself.

I force myself to concentrate in class. My teacher has her eye on me. With my behavior, I've been marked as the one to watch.

"Obayd!" she calls out.

I sit up straight. "Yes?"

"Come and solve the problem on the board." She holds out a stick of chalk. I rise from my spot on the floor and slide behind my classmates. I stare at the blackboard as I approach it.

She has written the number fifteen on the board.

"There are five people in your home, let's just say. And there are eighteen apples in a box." I nod, wanting her to know I am paying attention. My neck feels hot as I stand with my back to the rest of the students.

"You must divide the apples up so everyone has an equal share. How many will each person get and how many apples will be left over once you've divided them up?" She rubs her fingers together to get the chalk dust off.

"Speak as you solve the problem. Tell the class what you're doing."

The answer is simple. She's not really testing my math skills, I realize. She's testing *me*.

I bite my lip and think for a second. There is snickering behind me.

"If there are five people in the home . . . then . . . then . . ."

I press the stick of chalk to the board. My hand is shaking as I try to draw a line below the number she's written. Under the pressure the chalk lets out a hair-raising screech.

Hands fly up and cover ears. I cringe too.

"Class, that's enough!"

I wipe my forehead with the back of my hand. Are they staring at my legs? Are they imagining me with girl hair and realizing I'm a fraud?

"Obayd, we are waiting. Explain to the class how you would solve the problem."

I remind myself to breathe. All I can think is that there is a classroom full of eyes staring at me. I wonder how many of them know what I really am. I don't care about the apples. They can divide themselves.

"Forgive me, teacher."

"For what?"

I look her directly in the eye and place the piece of chalk in her hand. I hear whispers. She sees tears in my eyes and says nothing. She watches me return to my spot on the floor. The boy next to me looks at me, baffled. It's unheard-of to disobey a teacher. I brace myself.

"Class, what has happened here?" Her arms are folded across her chest.

Responses come flying in. I feel like I'm back on the field, getting knocked around by one-legged opponents.

"Obayd's not very good at math."

"He's scared of chalk."

"Maybe he's never had an apple."

Hands clap over mouths to dampen the laughter.

I want to shrink into my clothes like a turtle.

Our teacher takes control of the conversation. She slaps a ruler against the wall three times and clears her throat.

"Knowing something is useless if you cannot share what you know. It's almost like not knowing it at all. Obayd may very well be able solve the problem or even more complicated ones, but if he cannot tell us what he knows, we are left to think the worst."

There is quiet in the room. I am filled with hatred for this teacher, knowing she set me up to fail.

Recess comes and I am, for the first time, relieved to get out of my classroom. At least outside, I can move away from the gawkers. But I am barely outside the double doors when I feel something slam against me from behind. I stumble and can't catch myself. I'm on the ground.

I look back and see *W-I-Z-A-R-D-S*.

The other students are running past us. We are in an uneven face-off that no one else seems to notice.

"Get up," he says flatly. I can't see his eyes. They're hidden by the rim of his cap. From this close, I can see the red threads of the letters. They're wildly frayed and remind me of Meena's unruly hair.

"What do you want from me?" I blurt out angrily.

"Now, there's something," he says, his lips curled in a sly smile. He keeps his eyes on me as I get to my feet slowly.

"What's your problem? Just leave me alone." I brush my hands against the seat of my pants.

"What's your name?" He is unfazed by my attitude.

"Why should I tell you?"

"Because I bothered to ask. Has anyone else done that?"

No one else has.

"You're not having an easy time with it. That's pretty clear."

"With what?"

There it is again—that awkward feeling of being naked right here in the schoolyard. Instinctively, I hunch my shoulders forward and start to cave in on myself. My eyes focus on a pebble and my lips tighten into a knot.

"There it is. That's how I knew."

"Knew what?"

He leans in. His face is so close that I can see the spidery blood vessels in the whites of his eyes. He's about three years older than me and very intimidating. I pull back and turn my shoulder to him. If I can see that much of him, he can see even more of me. He smirks, hands on his hips. He is standing with his feet apart and his back straight. He is strong and confident and the opposite of me. I hate myself for being so meek.

"You're one."

I hold my breath. If he knows, I wish he would just say it. Maybe he's not sure and he wants me to admit it. I'm not going to give him the satisfaction. But I can't tell what he knows, and I'm not sure what to do.

"Get out of my face," I hiss and start to walk away. That seems to be all I know how to do today.

"I know what you are," he calls out behind me. The simple words make the short hairs on the back of my neck stand on end.

Eight

I think about him all weekend. I dread going back to school because I know what awaits me there. Inside the classroom things are bad, and outside the classroom things are even worse. I can't talk to my mother about anything. Just a few days ago, I overheard her telling one of my aunts that she wasn't sure if she'd done the right thing by making me a *bacha posh*. And the last time I tried to talk to her about being a *bacha posh*, she got so anxious that she didn't even seem to be making sense.

My sisters can't help me. Things have totally changed at home. My parents act as if they have no idea that I'm a girl. My mother's been sliding the biggest chunks of meat my way, and sometimes there's none left for my sisters. Alia whines and pouts, but Neela just shakes her head. I haven't washed any dishes or swept the floor in almost a month. The chores I used to do have been divided up among my sisters. This *bacha posh* thing has put a big wall between us.

Alia and Meena are in our bedroom. Meena is braiding Alia's hair as they sing.

"Meena, do you want to watch a movie?" There is electricity today, and it's been so long since we used our precious DVD player. When we were in Kabul, my sisters and I would borrow DVDs from anyone who had them and watch anything we could get our hands on. "You remember, Meena, the one where the father dresses up like an old woman so he can play with his kids."

"That movie was ridiculous," she says. She shoots me a skeptical look. "It made absolutely no sense. What man would ever dress up as a woman?"

Meena has a point but I don't want to admit it. Even if it's not at all a believable story, it made me laugh, especially when he was cooking and the stove set his fake breasts on fire.

"Oh, his voice was so funny. And his lady stockings!" Alia is giggling at the thought of it. Meena tugs at Alia's braid as if to rein her in.

"Fine, then what can we do? We've all finished our homework. Do you want to go sit in the courtyard? Maybe play jacks?"

"O-bayd," she says, making her mouth a perfect circle to say the first syllable of my name. It's dramatic, which is not usually her thing but I guess things can change. "If you want to go and play outside, then you should do it. *You* can do it. We're staying inside because we have to help Madar and listen in case our father needs anything, and we might have to help Neela, too. Since you don't have to do any of that stuff, you should go out and play whatever you want."

"Meena, what's wrong with you? I just asked if you wanted to do something." Meena is testy, like she's mad about something but won't say what it is so it comes out in different shapes and colors. I don't think she's really mad about me going outside into the courtyard. Alia looks over at Meena. She noticed too.

"I want to go—"

"Well, you can't!" Meena snaps. She shuts Alia down like a lid slammed on a pot. Alia hunches forward, her brows knitted together in frustration. The younger you are in a home, the worse you have it. There are just that many more people who can tell you what you should or shouldn't do. I don't know how many times I've heard my grandmother say, *God have mercy on the youngest in the house.*

"Meena, leave her alone!"

Meena glares at me.

"Stay out of it. We *sisters* are talking. Go and do your . . . your . . . your boy stuff!" Meena's seething as if this was something I chose.

Alia keeps her mouth shut. It's no fun being in the middle, either.

"Leave that meat for Obayd. Let Obayd go and play. Fold Obayd's clothes," she says, mimicking my mother. "As if we don't know that Obayd is not really OBAYD!"

"It's not my fault, Meena," I whisper. It is an awful feeling to think your sister is starting to hate you. "It's not what I wanted. I'm not even good at it."

I turn to leave the room. Just as I hit the hallway, I hear Meena call after me, but I don't go back even though she sounds like she's sorry for what she said.

The next morning, I'm back in class ready to be humiliated again, but my teacher does not call on me. She has a new victim, a boy not as timid as me but much worse at math. To act like you know the answer and then get it totally wrong is even worse, I think. It looks as though my teacher agrees.

I wish that could happen to the boy with the hat. I wish I could find a way to knock that smug look off his face. He knows what I am, but he did not scream it out to the others. Maybe he's telling the boys in whispers I don't hear. Maybe they'll all be staring at me when I get out there today. It won't take long for word to travel.

I hit the playground with the others. I think of what I might say if anyone asks me if I'm a girl. He's here. He sees me. No, he doesn't just see me. He's gloating over me, looking at me like I'm an algebra equation and he's already figured out the value of x. I want to scream.

"Hey, boy!" he yells out. He walks toward me. My hands ball up, not into fists, but into things I will use to cover my eyes if I start crying. With the way my sisters have been acting, I'm starting to feel really lonely.

"Why did you turn around?" he asks me.

"Didn't you call me?"

"You answer to *boy*? Are you a boy?" His tone is sarcastic, teasing, and there's no perfect reply to his question.

"What do you want? Why do you have such a problem with me?"

He laughs, big enough that I see his teeth and the pink of his mouth. I hate that I'm shorter. Even when I'm not on the ground, I'm always looking up at this boy. I lower my eyes to his knees.

"I'm not the one who has a problem with you," he says snidely.

"You're not? Then who is?"

"You. *You're* the one that has a problem with you."

"Stupid. What do you know?" My words sound ridiculously small, like I'm throwing pebbles at a mountain.

"Little boy," he whispers. "I don't think any part of you is a boy."

He gives me a quick shove. I'm not expecting it and fall back a step. He grunts.

"You see how easily you fall? You stand like you're not sure you should be here. Are you supposed to be here, Obayd?"

"You . . . you know my name."

"Yes, I know your name."

"How do you know my name?" I'm puzzled. He is older than me. Not enough that we can't play *ghursai* together, but enough that he shouldn't care to know my name or anything else about me. Other than being someone to knock over on the schoolyard, I should be invisible to him. But I'm not.

"And why are you staring at my feet? Look at *me*." With a quick chuck under my chin, he flips my gaze upward. Our eyes meet.

His are bold, shiny. Mine are fluttering, frightened little things.

"You just sit there and let things happen to you. If we were playing soccer instead of *ghursai*, you would look more like the ball than a player."

My face burns. I'm feeling exposed—like he can see my insides from where he stands.

I should walk away. But I can't because every word

from his mouth is true, and it's hard to walk away from someone who knows me so well. Part of me wants to know what he'll say next, as much as it might hurt.

"Don't you have anything to say? Where's your voice?" he mocks. "If you don't have anything to say, maybe you should run home and play with your sister's dolls."

Was he talking about Alia?

"What do you know about my sister?" My head is spinning. My breaths are shallow and tight. I get the words out with a whole lot of effort. "Why do you think you know me?"

The boy grabs my shoulders with both of his hands. His fingers are so strong, I can feel them pressing into the ligaments that connect my arm to my body. I think he might throw me to the ground and walk away, but he doesn't. Instead, he brings his face to my ear and whispers a truth that will be mine and his.

"I *know* you because I *am* you."

Nine

I know *you because I* am *you.*

I hadn't expected him to say that.

My mother watches me. When school started I dragged my feet. I wanted to go but wasn't sure what people would say to me. All that changed after that boy breathed that one heavy sentence into my ear.

I have to see him again.

My mother tries to decipher my new enthusiasm. She hasn't seen me this eager to go to school since we were in Kabul, but I was a girl then and our family was different.

My sisters and I leave the house together. It's chilly and I'm glad I have a boys' sweater on over my shirt. At the end of the main road, Neela turns left to go toward her school. When we were in Kabul, my parents had started talking about her going to college. There's nothing after high school in this village, though, and Neela knows that. In the village, we take what we can get. Water, electricity, schooling—none of it's guaranteed.

I duck into my classroom. My teacher already seems to have lost interest in me. I'm just another student to her now. The boy next to me is sharpening his pencil.

We're instructed to recite our multiplication tables. I don't mind the math, so the morning goes by quickly.

Recess comes and I'm the first one out the door. The sun is bright and heat radiates from the earth. I look for him, but he's not in the yard. I scan from left to right, searching for figures of the right height, looking for a blue hat and reminding myself he might not be wearing it today. When my eyes fall on him, I feel my heart pause.

He . . . Should I call him he or she? He, I decide, because that's what he wants to be. He is walking with his three friends. I've seen them playing soccer, reading magazines, and kicking at each other as if they were kung fu masters. Having seen one or two American movies starring Bruce Lee, the gravity-defying actor, I am ready to tell them they look amateurish. Their kicks are askew, their arms choppy. I watch the boy in the blue hat. He manages to catch his friend's foot as it flies toward him. He laughs and pushes the foot to the right, sending his friend spinning. I feel myself start to smile.

Not bad . . . for a girl.

I watch his body. Even though he is about three years older than me, his body is not. I don't see knobs on his chest. I don't know what else to look for. If he hadn't told me, I never would have known. He moves as the rest of them move. I wonder how he's trained his body to do that. I feel meek and flimsy watching him.

I move closer to his friends. Are they girls too? I stare at them, trying to analyze the angles of their jaws, the shapes of their hands. I narrow in on their upper lips and eyebrows, hoping hair will separate reality from disguise. In the end, I'm not sure either way. If the boy with the blue cap managed to trick me, everyone is a question mark.

"Hey! Hey, you! What are you staring at?"

I'm startled when I realize one of the boys has noticed me. I run my fingers along the bark of a mulberry tree that shades the schoolyard and turn my eyes to the ground.

"Don't act like you didn't hear me!"

The blue hat boy turns around and realizes I'm the gawker his friend has caught. I raise my hand and shrug my shoulders in a messy gesture of admission and apology. I don't know if he understands, but the blue-hat boy's face goes serious. He says something to his friends and walks in my direction.

"What are you doing?" he says when he gets close

enough that I can hear him.

"I was hoping . . . I wanted to talk to you some more because . . . Did you mean what you said?"

He raises his eyebrows. He wants me to say it.

I take a deep breath in and exhale my question, careful to lower my voice even though there's no one within yards of us.

"Are you a *bacha posh*?"

"Of course I am," he says with a funny smile. His voice is softer than it was the last time we spoke. Something heavy in the air between us disappears. I can't help but stare at his lips and his face. Just for a second, I can see him as a girl. I picture him with long hair and his face makes total sense. "But I'm not new to this like you are. You better get used to it quickly or you'll attract a lot of attention—and it won't be good attention."

I bite my lip. I know he's right. Several kids look at me with curiosity. Others don't notice me at all. Then there are the rare ones that stare outright, like they've spotted an extinct animal.

"What should I do?"

"You're a *bacha posh*. Forget everything else and be a boy."

"But I've been a girl my whole life. How can I forget everything?"

"It's not as hard as you might think." He fidgets with

his hat, adjusts the rim so it shields his eyes from the sun. "I think I can help you."

"What's your name?" I ask him.

"Rahim." His grin is mischievous.

"Rahim," I repeat. "And before?"

"Rahima," he says. His grin fades. Her grin fades? What should I call this person? I figure he won't like me very much if I refer to him as a girl in any way, even if it's just in my head. I make up my mind that Rahim will be a boy and nothing else. "But now that name sounds like it belongs to someone else. I don't think I would even turn my head if I heard someone calling *Rahima* on the street."

Is it possible to leave your name behind? Could I ever *not* be Obayda? I can't imagine it. That might be what's holding me back from being like Rahim.

We sit on an old tire left on the side of the schoolyard. Rahim is wearing jeans thinned at the knees and a polo T-shirt. I'm wearing cargo pants meant for a boy younger than me, so my ankles stick out.

"Was it hard for you?"

He does not ask me what I mean. He does not shy away from the question. He knows why I'm asking. It's nice being able to talk to someone who gets me.

I know you because I am you.

"In the beginning I was a girl dressed in boy clothes. That was really hard. I didn't know how to act. I wanted to cross my legs and fix my head scarf." He laughs at the thought of it. I laugh too, trying to imagine what Rahim would look like with a head scarf tied over his *W-I-Z-A-R-D-S* hat. It's as silly as the American actor dressed like a grandmother.

"But then I realized I couldn't be a girl dressed in boy clothes. I had to *be* a boy wearing my clothes. This is the best thing. You can wake up and throw on those ugly, too-short pants and run to school. You should jump up and down and be loud when you want to be and eat all you can. You should tell people what you think and score goals and let your father look at you like you're the future president of Afghanistan."

"How do I do that?"

Rahim stares at me. He bites his lip. I start to regret my question. I feel like he's about to pick me apart in that painful way that he does.

"Stand up," he says. His voice goes from delicate to rough in no time.

I do it, wondering for a split second if I have tire treads on my backside.

"Do you remember what I told you the other day? Look at the way you stand, the way you hide your eyes. Being a boy is not all in your pants. It's in your head. It's in your shoulders." He's jabbing at me to make his point.

"Cut it out," I mutter.

"What?" Rahim cocks his head to the side and flicks my earlobe. I swipe at his hand, but I'm too late and get nothing but air.

"I said cut it out!" I'm annoyed. Rahim has a way of spoiling conversations with his antics. I don't want to be his punching bag.

He palms my forehead and pushes me toward the ground.

This time I kick at him. I fall to the ground but manage to bring my foot to his shin on my way down. He lets out a howl and claps triumphantly.

"Better," he says. "Stand tall. Stick your chin out like you're daring me to hit it. Set your feet apart. You've got boy parts, don't forget. Keep your palms open and let your arms swing while you walk. If you hear something behind you, turn around and look for it. When you run, slap your whole foot on the ground, not just your toes. Are you carrying eggs in your pockets?"

Eggs?

"No? Then don't walk like you are. Run like you're not afraid of cracking any shells!"

He points at my feet, nudges my chin and my elbows. I listen to his words and feel my body loosen. It's easier to breathe. Why is that?

"What else?"

"You're a boy, not a *bacha posh*, Obayd. If you get that,

there is nothing else. You know your weaknesses now, don't you? Boys aren't supposed to have weaknesses. Boys are built of rock and metal. We eat meat and show our teeth."

"And girls?"

"Girls are made of flower petals and paper bags. They eat berries and sip tea like something might jump out of the hot water and bite them."

I was torn—half of me angry at his depiction of girls and the other half of me proud not to be one for now.

"I don't know if that's true," I say. I don't want to contradict him, but I've never thought of myself as a paper bag. "Tell me honestly, you're happy being a *bacha posh*?"

"Is that even a question? Why would I want to be anything else?" He looks at me as if I've got potatoes for ears. "You're new to this, which means you know what it is to be a girl. Was it anything worth being?"

I'm not sure how to answer. He starts to stroll the length of the schoolyard. I follow, trying to synchronize my pace with his. Left foot, right foot, left foot . . . his legs are longer than mine and I fall off beat often.

"Me? I didn't like it one bit. I didn't realize I had a choice or I would have asked my mother to change me years ago. Do you know what I used to do when I was a girl? Help in the kitchen, help with the laundry, serve tea to guests, run from the boys in the streets . . ."

73

I did all those things just a few weeks ago. Did I hate it? Maybe I did. Maybe it was all awful and I didn't know any better. Maybe everything had been blurry till this exact moment, this one conversation.

"It just feels so strange right now," I confess.

"It'll get easier. It sort of just happens. For me, it happened the day I got this hat." He points to his blue cap. "The day I got this hat, I knocked over four boys playing *ghursai* and stayed on my feet for the whole game. I haven't fallen once as long as I have this hat on. It's like a good-luck charm. Stick close by and it'll rub off on you too."

Rahim looks over at his friends, who are heading back into the school. I feel lucky to have this exciting new friend. If we were girls, we wouldn't have ever met. It's only because we're a special kind of boy that we have found each other. Maybe his hat has rubbed off on me already. When he turns back to me, I can see the girl in his eyes. He takes my hand and squeezes it between his long, thin fingers.

"Nobody helped me when I first changed. But I'm going to help you. We'll be like brothers!" He laughs. I laugh too—not because he's funny, but because I'm happy.

He always seems to have a look on his face, and now that I can stare at him straight on and not out of the corner of my eye, I can see what the look really is. Rahim looks like he can do anything.

Ten

I've been a *bacha posh* for four weeks and five days, and I've finally settled into my class. Sometimes a game of *ghursai* starts up at recess. Rahim and I play on the same field but never on the same team because pairing up might call attention to what we have in common. I'm a little better than I was during that first game, which is good because being friends with Rahim doesn't mean anything once the *attack* command rings out. I can get almost halfway to the other team's side, but I'm still one of the first to be knocked out. Every single time.

I've gone from thinking Rahim was out to get me to being best friends with him. He even introduced me to his friends, Ashraf and Abdullah, and they like me, even though I'm younger than them.

Rahim and I meet after school a few days a week. My sisters shoot me looks over their shoulders as they trudge home. I'm allowed to stay out for a while. Now that I have Rahim to talk to, I like having this extra time, and I use it. The distance between us and my sisters widens. Once they're too far to hear, we can talk about the things that are about us and only us.

"One little letter fell off the back end of my name and my world changed. It's the smallest little letter, barely even a sound. Rahim . . . Rahima. See? If you say it fast enough, you could miss it. Who ever thought such a tiny little letter could make such a big difference?"

Rahim has a lot he wants to teach me, things he couldn't tell anyone who isn't just like him. I'm ready to listen because no one else will tell me things—not even my mother.

"How long have you been a boy?" I have so many questions to ask Rahim. Sometimes I forget the questions I thought up overnight, but it works out fine because there's always something else to ask.

"I've been a boy since I was nine years old. Not that different from you, actually."

"You don't have any brothers?"

"If I did, I wouldn't be what I am," he says simply. When it's just the two of us, his voice is much softer than it is around the boys. "I'm the middle sister in my family. I've got two sisters older than me and two younger than me. Sometimes my father would pull us out of school. He didn't like that boys were following us home or teasing us. He thought people would start talking."

I know what he means by that. Getting attention is not a good thing for girls in our village. Things were the same in Kabul, too. Even just a little attention from a stranger could get a girl dragged into the house so fast her feet might get left outside. It's almost as if all girls are born knowing what could happen, so we try to move around outside like ghosts—keeping our voices low, our footsteps light, and our eyes to the ground.

"So my aunt came up with this idea to make me a *bacha posh*. Now I come to school and no one bothers me. No one follows me. I even work after school."

His chest puffs out as he shares that last bit with me.

"This was my aunt's idea too," I admit. "What work do you do?"

"Do you know the electronics shop on the same block as the baker? I help out there. I'm learning a lot."

That seems awfully grown-up to me. I wonder if the job is harder than he's making it sound. I know some kids who work in shops have it really rough, especially the ones who don't go to school at all. I'm glad we're not so poor that I have to carry bricks or sacks of rice. Fixing radios might be interesting, but I doubt I'd be lucky enough to find something so professional-sounding.

"Do you know any other boys like us?" That's what I call *bacha posh*es now—*boys like us.*

"Lots," he says, his eyes wide for emphasis. They've got the unmistakable sparkle of a girl, but I guess most people don't pay close attention.

"Lots? Like how many? In this school?" I look up and down the dirt street. Have I missed spotting them?

"No, no. Not here. But in other neighborhoods and in other villages."

I wonder what it would be like to meet them or if I would even recognize one the way Rahim recognized me. I think I would now that I've met Rahim. Until I got to know him, I found it hard to believe another *bacha posh* could really exist. But knowing there are two of us makes me look at all the boys around me and wonder if I'll spot another.

Rahim adjusts the cap on his head, which makes me think of something I noticed the first day I saw my new friend.

"Hey, Rahim, what does *why-zar-dis* mean?"

Rahim spins around to look at me. He looks confused. "What did you say?"

"Your hat. I've been wondering what *why-zar-dis* means." My words are slower this time.

Rahim erupts in thick laughter. It seems to be coming from somewhere deep in his body.

My face gets hot. I know for certain I've said the wrong thing. I want him to stop laughing. I fold my arms across my chest and wait for him to stop. When he doesn't, I kick his calf.

"Ow! What did you do that for?" he whines, rubbing his leg. He's not laughing anymore. "Come on, Obayd. It was funny. Don't be so sensitive."

"Don't be such a jerk."

Rahim gets like this sometimes. I know it's because he's older than me and he's been a boy longer, but it's still annoying. He's like Khala Aziza, my *Let me tell you what you should do* aunt.

"It's *wizards*," he says plainly, which is just about as good as an apology. "My cousin in America sent me this hat. It's a basketball team over there."

"Oh."

We keep walking. It's late afternoon and Rahim is walking me home—something he always does. He says it's because he likes walking, but I know he's looking out for me too. I really like having a best friend who's older than me. Rahim looks out for me the way my oldest sister, Neela, does, but it's also different—more like an older brother, I guess.

"Does the name mean something?"

"No. I mean, I don't know." Rahim says it quickly. It's not like him not to have an answer. It occurs to me that he shouldn't have laughed so hard at the way I said it.

When we reach the metal door of my home, we pause.

"Do you want to come in?" I ask him because I know that's what my mother would do if she were walking home with a friend. I can only imagine what my sisters would say to Rahim. They've seen him from a distance at school, far enough that they wouldn't ever suspect his true identity. But sitting next to me, my sisters would recognize him quickly, knowing I wouldn't bring an actual boy home. I picture my sisters with antennae buzzing on their heads. The image is so funny, I have to bite my lip not to laugh. It's too much to explain to Rahim, who is carefully considering our front door. He tries to see over the clay wall that hides our courtyard and home from view. He takes a deep breath.

"I think I'd better get home," he says. "My mother worries if I stay out too late."

I nod. I was just being polite anyway.

A mother and daughter walk hurriedly past us, the young girl's hand held tightly by her mother's. Their skirts are long, their head scarves draped over their shoulders and falling past their hips. Their feet shuffle as they try to move quickly. It is late in the afternoon and the streets are starting to quiet.

There's something else I've been wanting to ask Rahim. Something I probably shouldn't be thinking about now, but I can't help it.

"Rahim, can I ask you something? What's going to happen to you? When are they going to change you back?"

Rahim's face gets really serious. His eyelids lower and his lips tighten. He stuffs his hands deep into his pockets and I worry that I've asked something I shouldn't have.

"Never," my best friend says with so much fire that I get a little nervous for him. "I'll never be a girl again."

Eleven

There's a yelping noise.

"Get away from him!" Rahim calls out. We're walking home from school, blowing on our hands to keep them warm. It's starting to get really cold out. Winter's not far away.

I turn to see what Rahim's yelling about. Two older boys are chasing after a stray dog. They corner him in an alley and one boy picks up a small stone. The dog's a mud-covered mutt with patchy hair. He's cowering, looking for a way out.

"Leave him alone!" Rahim yells again. He charges at the boys. They turn, surprised. I can see their faces become knotted with anger.

"Rahim, wait! What are you doing?"

He ignores me. He's already in front of the dog, who is backing away from Rahim, too. He's not sure if he's got any friends.

"Leave the dog alone, you brutes!" Rahim's hands are balled up. One of the boys takes a step toward him and gives him a shove. Rahim shoves him back. I'm terrified but run to my friend's side.

"Stop!" I yell. I don't know what else I can do.

"What's your problem? Is this dog your sister or something?" The boy jeers.

"No, he's the child your mother wished she'd had instead of you," Rahim shoots back. I'm impressed. And nervous.

The dog senses his opportunity and scampers away.

The boy swings at Rahim's head, but my friend ducks backward and the boy stumbles to the ground. He comes after Rahim again. Rahim kicks at his leg and the boy grabs his shin, howling in pain. His friend looks at us and charges at Rahim. Without thinking, I stick my leg out and trip him. He falls flat on his face. Rahim looks at me. He doesn't have to say it. I know what he's thinking.

We run as fast as we can. Our girl legs are light and quick. The boys chase us down one street, but when we make our second turn, they give up. Once we're sure we've lost them, we rest against a wall and catch our breath.

"I can't believe you did that!" Rahim laughs.

"I can't believe it either," I admit.

"That dog looked so sad. I didn't want to see them hit it with a rock. Thanks for backing me up."

"You're my friend, Rahim. I wouldn't leave you to fight those boys alone."

"You fought a boy and won, Obayd." Rahim grabs my hands excitedly. "Isn't that great? Doesn't it feel really good? We took down a couple of boys! Let him explain to his friends that his hands and face got all scraped up when he got taken down by a couple of girl-boys."

This is one of our best days so far as boys.

I enter the living room, still feeling really good. As usual, my father's not there.

"Obayd, good. You're finally here."

"*Salaam*, Mother."

"My son, take a plate of food to your father, would you? He didn't want to eat earlier, but maybe his appetite will pick up if he sees you."

I toss my backpack against the wall.

My sisters are sitting on the floor cushions. Their notebooks are splayed across the burgundy carpet like butterfly wings.

"When is he going to come out of that room?" I ask. I kind of want to tell him what I just did, though I don't know what he'll say about it.

The leaves on the chinar tree outside have gone from green to orange and yellow and red and now they're falling to the ground. The season is shifting and changing, just like me. I have both hands on my hips and my chin nudged forward in my best boy pose. My sisters look at me. Meena rolls her eyes, Alia giggles, and Neela pretends not to notice.

"This is not easy for him, Obayd." My mother sounds tired. "Your father loved putting on his uniform every morning. He felt good when he was working. He earned money that fed us, bought our clothes, and kept us in a decent apartment. He doesn't have that now. And when you have no reason to leave the house, you have no way of coming home happy."

"But it's not his fault."

"Of course it isn't. But it's hard to tell a one-legged man that it's time to stand up."

I think I know how my father feels. Rahim seems to think we can stand like boys, but sometimes I wonder if he and I have everything it takes to do that.

There is a large plate of rice and lentils and a bowl of curried vegetables. I pour the saucy mix over the pile of rice and pick out a spoon and fork. I take it into the bedroom, balancing everything so I can knock on the door frame and announce myself. There isn't an actual door, just an opening where a door should be, which is kind of like my father—there's just empty pant where his leg should be.

My father is curled up on his side, his face to the window so I can't see it.

"Padar," I say softly. I take two steps in. The explosion in Kabul blew out one of my father's eardrums, too, so he can't hear very well. I make my voice a little louder. "Padar?"

"Mm. What is it?"

"I've brought you some dinner."

"Not hungry."

"Mother says you haven't eaten yet."

"I'll eat when I'm hungry."

I stand there for a moment and feel myself getting angry with my father. I know he's missing a leg, but what about the rest of him? He's got hands and arms and a whole other leg that he could be using. It's like everything good, all his smiles and jokes, were in that leg, and when the bomb went off it sent all of it flying away.

Is he going to stay like this forever?

I blurt something out before I have a chance to give it a second thought.

"When are you going to get up?"

My father isn't fazed by the frustration in my voice.

"Padar, why don't you sit with us? Why don't you even listen to your radio anymore?"

When he doesn't answer, I feel myself getting angrier and then scared that he's so mad he won't even talk to me anymore.

"Padar?"

"Didn't you hear your mother, Obayd?" he says in a flat voice. "You can't tell a one-legged man to stand up."

Twelve

It's the end of the school year and the start of a three-month break from classes. I've always liked winter, even if it does come with some problems. In Kabul, the snow would mix with dirt and turn the streets into a brown, slushy disaster. It's doing the same thing here in our village. I don't mind because there's a lot of good stuff that comes with the snow too, like snow games and holidays and air that's crisp.

It is my first winter as a boy. Now that I've been one for almost two months, I can't wait for the adventures this new season will bring.

Rahim knocks on my door with his friends Abdullah and Ashraf. Rahim told me that they've always known he's not a full boy and that they never seemed to care. While that makes them some of the nicest guys I've ever met, I still feel a little jealous when they're around because it means Rahim splits his attention three ways and I don't get the biggest share. Rahim is Abdullah's best friend too. What I really like about Rahim is that even when he's got all of us around him, he still makes me feel like I'm more than just a regular friend. I feel really good about that, especially since I'm three years younger.

Since we don't have school, Rahim invites me to play in the snow with them. I put on an extra shirt and a sweater to keep me warm under my coat. It's so cold out that my nose starts to run and my eyes tear. My face is a wet mess, which makes me feel even colder. I'm still happy, though.

I follow the boys into the street. There's nearly a foot of snow on the ground and it's still coming down. We are jogging down the street, but our feet get stuck in the snow and we have to make tall, high steps to get anywhere. My toes are starting to go numb when I feel a whack on my left shoulder. Abdullah is grinning.

"Hey!" I call out. Before I can say another word, I feel a thump against my chest. Ashraf teams up with Abdullah. Rahim moves closer to me to even things out. He's already rolling a snowball in his hands and taking aim.

"Don't just stand there, Obayd," he yells at me. "Fight back!"

My snowballs are mostly fluff and land at Ashraf's feet or fly over Abdullah's shoulder instead of making any contact. Rahim is really good and makes enough hits that it almost seems like an even fight when it really isn't.

I watch the boys and learn a few tricks. Abdullah digs out snow closer to the ground so it's already more packed. Ashraf and Rahim rub their bare hands on the snowball's surface, which makes it ice over. Those are the snowballs that sting through the two shirts, the sweater, and the coat I'm wearing.

The day after my first snowball fight, I count seven purple welts on my body. They are round and hurt when I press on them, but I feel pretty good about them. They're like badges of honor.

Two weeks into winter, Rahim doesn't have to do all the work in our snow battles. My snowballs are deadly.

On another day, we wander through town and find a group of older boys. They've started a fire in a big tin can using sticks, newspaper, and oil. Abdullah is with them and waves us over. They make room for us and we stand in a tight circle, warming our hands over the flames. I like the way the fire snaps and jumps. I also like being part of this circle, even if I am the shortest one here. With my coat and knit hat, I blend in even with the older boys.

The boys have collected loose papers and leaflets to

feed the fire. I notice a page of cartoon drawings and English writing. There's a word that catches my eye because I've been staring at those letters for the past two months. *W-I-Z-A-R-D-S.* Just like Rahim's cap.

Above the word is a cartoon drawing of an old man with a wrinkled face and a long beard. There are other cartoon drawings with words underneath them. It's some kind of booklet used to teach English. Our school in Kabul used similar ones.

Rahim's standing right next to me so I elbow him. He's talking to Abdullah when I interrupt.

"What is it?" he asks.

"Look at this." I point to the picture and the word below it. "Like your hat. I thought you said it was the name of a basketball team?"

Rahim looks at the page in my hand.

"It is . . ." he mutters. I can tell the picture doesn't make any sense to him, either.

"Why would they name a basketball team after old men with beards? This guy looks like a great-grandfather."

Rahim has this look on his face that tells me whatever he's about to say is probably not true—or at least not totally true.

"Because . . . they probably named the team after some old guy that used to play basketball when he was young. You know, like the way the Gardens of Babur are named after Babur." Rahim points at the black-and-white drawing I'm holding. "This guy's name must be Wizard."

One of the older boys overhears us. He sees the skeptical look on my face.

"What are you two looking at?"

"It's nothing," Rahim says, and rubs his hands together over the fire. He shivers a little. "Just some pictures."

This is my chance to get some older boys to tell me what they think. They might know something Rahim doesn't.

"Here, look at this," I say, passing the paper over to the boy on the opposite side of the circle. I'm careful not to reach directly over the flames so my coat doesn't catch fire. The boy, who is old enough to have a thin mustache, takes the page from me. "Rahim says that's an old man who used to play basketball."

The boy laughs.

"Basketball? You don't know what a wizard is, do you?" he asks Rahim.

Rahim's face gets hot with anger.

"Yes, I do! It's the name of a basketball team," he barks, pointing at his hat. "My cousin from America told me so."

"It might be that, too, but a wizard is a magician. He's an old guy who can cast spells or make things disappear. Do you really think this guy looks like an athlete?" He rolls up the paper and tosses it into the fire. Rahim and I stare as the flames turn its edges black and eat it up.

A magician. Rahim's got a magician's hat?

Rahim's hat is suddenly a lot more interesting than it has been. Maybe that's why I was drawn to it when I first met him.

Rahim and I walk home together, since his home is not far from mine.

"That's cool, isn't it? Your hat says *magician*."

Rahim nods. He's forgiven me (mostly) for pointing out to all the older boys that he had no idea what he was talking about earlier.

"Maybe the hat gives you some special powers. If I had special powers, I'd turn myself into a basketball player. Or maybe I'd make huge platters of food appear out of nowhere. What would you do if you could be a magician? Would you turn yourself into a bird? A tiger?"

"Nah," Rahim says. He looks up at the rim of his cap. His ears and the top of his nose are bright red with cold. "I'd do something else."

"Like what?"

Rahim doesn't say another word. He doesn't have to. I know what he would turn himself into if he had the power.

Thirteen

Rahim and I sit on a low wall at the end of the market. There wasn't much work in the electronics shop today, so the shopkeeper sent Rahim off early. Today is the first day we can be outside without our fingers going numb from cold. There is still snow and slush on the ground, but spring is only a few weeks away and we'll be back in school soon. It's hard to believe how fast the three-month winter break has gone by.

"Rahim, look at that!" I point to an older man walking down the street. His head is covered in a wool hat and he is hunched forward as he walks away from us. He has a tall walking stick in his right hand and hobbles a bit.

"That man? What about him?" Rahim's not sure what's caught my eye.

"Don't you see what he's walking with?"

"Yeah, it's a stick. What's the big deal?"

"It's not just a stick, Rahim. Look at it."

My friend takes a closer look. It is a tall stick, almost as tall as the man himself. His eyes move downward until he realizes what's caught my attention. Halfway down the stick, there's a cut-off branch with a small padded ledge on it. On the ledge rests the man's stump—a folded-up pant leg where his knee should be. My mouth hangs open to see how comfortably this man walks, with a little swing to his march as he sets the crutch down and then takes a step with his left half leg.

"Whoa!"

I'm on my feet. "Yeah, isn't that cool?"

"I've never seen a stick like that before."

"Rahim, my father needs a stick like that. I bet he could finally walk around with something like that man has."

"Where do you think he got it?"

I'm already running to find out the answer to Rahim's question. It's not as easy as I thought it might be to catch up to the one-legged man. Rahim's right behind me.

"Excuse me, mister," I call out. I'm close enough that he should hear me, but he doesn't stop. The man has a bulky jacket on over his tunic and pants. He's got a plastic bag in his left hand, heavy with something he's just purchased from the market.

"Mister, please, just one moment!" I am right behind him. He plods on. From this close, I can see the padding his stump sits on. I watch how easily he moves with this stick, and my heart leaps. I wish I could take a picture and show my father.

"You dropped something from your bag, mister! I think this is yours," Rahim calls out. The old man comes to an abrupt stop and turns around. Nothing has dropped out of the bag, so I shoot Rahim a look. My empty-handed friend winks at me.

"What's fallen from my bag?" the man grumbles through a scraggly beard. He lifts his bag and sees no holes. This makes him even grumpier. "What are you bothering with me for? Don't you have any respect?"

"Excuse me, mister. I didn't mean to disturb you, but can you please tell me where you got your walking stick?"

"It's none of your business," he mutters. He turns to get back on his way. I hurry to walk alongside him. I'm guessing he's like my father and doesn't want to talk about his leg. Maybe he doesn't talk much at home, either.

"Please, mister, I know you are upset about your leg, but I just—"

"Upset about my leg?" Now I've really gotten his attention. He stops and takes a step toward me. I take a step back. "What does my leg have to do with anything?"

"I thought that's why you're so grumpy."

The man throws his head back and laughs, but not in a happy or funny way. Rahim is right next to me, and I'm really glad for that.

"I'm grumpy because it's cold and two little . . ." He takes a closer look at us and ignores that we might not be boys. That's what people do, I've learned as a *bacha posh*. "Two little boys are chasing after an old man to tease him about his groceries falling out of his bag."

"Oh."

"But that's what you think when you look at me, eh? You see only what's missing. You don't see the rest of me."

I could apologize, but I'd rather keep my mouth shut. I'm afraid I'll only upset him more.

"And what if I did the same? What if I look at you and see only what you're missing? Would you like that, *little boys*?"

He's looking at both of us. Rahim's so close to me I can feel his breath on the back of my ear. We get it.

"Mister, my father lost his leg. I want to see him walking in the street like you. Please, I just want to know where you got this walking stick."

He is quiet for a second.

"What does he use to get around now?"

"Nothing." I shrug. "He doesn't go anywhere at all. I

think if he had a walking stick like yours maybe he would."

The man's voice is much gentler now. I am not as nervous.

"This stick," he says looking down at the pole in his right hand, "is nothing much, but it's the best thing I've found. Look at it. Nothing but a long branch. My son made it for me. He made this little ledge here and covered it with cloth."

There's a Y-shaped fork in the branch and right in the crook of that fork sits a carved little ledge wrapped thick with fabric. It is a really simple thing, actually. I look at Rahim, who breaks out into a smile.

"Thanks, mister! Sorry we bothered you!" I am bursting with energy. I grab Rahim's sleeve and start jogging back down the road, where a patch of chinar trees grows away from the small shops and stands.

The old man shoos us off with a chuckle.

"Obayd, you think we can do it?"

"Rahim, I think we can do anything!"

Fourteen

We walk through the trees. I look up through the branches for one that would work. It's Rahim who spots it. My friend's got a good eye for these things.

"That one there!"

I see the branch he's pointing at. With the old man's walking stick fresh in my mind, I can see it's the perfect shape. It's long and straight and thick enough for a man's hand to wrap around. There are smaller branches shooting off in different directions, but some of them are thick enough that they can be the fork where the little bench will sit.

There's only one problem. The branch is about halfway up a very, very tall tree.

"How are we supposed to get up there, Rahim?"

"We've got to climb up. Then we've got to cut the branch down. I don't know how we're going to do that part."

"I think I know how to do it!" I'm nervous, but I have to make this work. "Give me a boost."

Rahim locks his hands together, making a step for me. I put my right foot on his hands and grab on to the lowest branch I can reach. I pull myself up and get my belly onto the branch, then my knee.

"I did it!" I call out. I stay as close to the trunk as I can. I'm about six feet off the ground and don't want to fall off. The branch is still another eight feet over my head. I reach up and grab on to the next big branch.

"Be careful," Rahim shouts from below. "If you break your leg, I'm not carrying you home."

"Very funny," I mutter. I know I shouldn't look down, but I do. My stomach does a flip-flop when I see how far up I am. I like climbing trees, but I've never gone this high up before. I climb, higher and higher, until I've got my hands around the branch that's perfect because it's thick and straight. I tug on it, as hard as I can, but it doesn't budge.

"What's the matter?"

"I can't get it to break off," I say. "I'm going to try something else."

I take a deep breath, but not before I look down once more. My head spins to see how small Rahim looks. This might be a mistake.

I grunt, pulling myself to the next branch. I get my right leg up but am afraid to pull up my left since my weight might throw me all the way over and off the branch. Rahim isn't saying anything, which I know means he's really nervous for me. My palms are sweaty.

I move slowly, bringing my left leg up carefully so I won't topple over in any direction.

I stop where I am. I'm right above the branch I want for my father's walking stick, but it's too early to celebrate. With my arms around the trunk of the tree in a giant hug, I kick at the branch right where it comes off the trunk. It doesn't budge.

"Ugh!" I really want to be back on the ground. I've discovered, being this high up for the first time in my life, that I'm very afraid of heights.

"You can do it, Obayd! I know you can kick stronger than that!"

Kick, kick, kick.

I hear a snap.

The branch is nearly knocked off! It's hanging by a skinny piece, like a loose tooth. I give it one last determined kick.

Crack!

Rahim, who's been staring up, throws his hands over his head and runs for cover. The branch crashes to the ground.

"You did it, Obayd! Now get down!"

I shimmy my way back down, finding branches to step on to get myself lower and lower until I'm close enough to the ground that I can jump down without thinking I'm going to break a few bones.

Rahim throws his arm around my shoulders and squeezes me. He's got the walking stick in his left hand. It's so perfect.

"You did it! And thanks for aiming this thing right at my head, buddy."

"You could have made yourself useful and caught it."

We can make jokes now that I'm back on the ground.

"How tall is your father? We need to pick the right height for that ledge."

I imagine my father standing next to me and point out how far up I think the ledge should be. We snap off that branch, leaving enough of a Y to hold the bench. We snap off the extra offshoots right where they are attached to the branch. Already, the stick is looking like the old man's.

Rahim's got an idea for the ledge. We go back to the market, where we find some beat-up cardboard boxes near the shops. He takes one and tears off a bunch of rectangles that would fit the fork of the walking stick.

"That looks like it'll work!"

I start to tear off pieces too, to match the ones he's made. We stack about ten of them to make a piece that's thick enough to give support. We tear out little notches on either side to make room for the branches, and it sits perfectly in place.

"Now we just need to wrap these in some cloth to bind them together and it'll be perfect! Your father's going to love it."

I break out into a smile. This crutch could be it. This could be that thing that my father needs to get him out of his room and back into life. He might just try it out and realize he can get up on his own. That's what I want to believe.

But deep down inside there's a tiny part of me that's worried my father won't love it at all and that when he looks at it, he'll see nothing but a dead tree branch.

Fifteen

We hid the unfinished stick at Rahim's home until I found the scraps of fabric I needed in my mother's sewing basket. Yesterday, I wrapped the little cardboard ledge in layers of brown velvet until it was soft with padding. I pinned the fabric on the underside of the ledge so it would hold.

Rahim agreed to come with me to give the walking stick to my father. We're both kind of nervous about this. He's never been inside my home before, and I think it's because he doesn't want me inside his. I know about his mother and sisters, but I've also noticed he doesn't talk much about his father, even when I talk about mine. As a friend, I'm not sure if I should be asking him why that is or if I should let it be. I let it be, though it's probably not because I want to be a good friend. It's probably because I'm too afraid of what he might tell me.

Rahim's standing with the walking stick in his right hand. He tries to put his bent knee on the ledge, but it's too tall for him to rest it there. He stands on his tiptoes and barely reaches.

"I think it'll work. You did a good job with the material."

"Thanks. I don't know if that pin is going to hold the fabric, but I think it looks almost as good as that old man's stick."

"Are you kidding? It looks so much better than his. Have you ever heard of a velvet walking stick? It's the kind of stuff kings probably use."

I don't know of any one legged kings, but Rahim's energy is contagious. I start to feel flutters in my stomach. I'm anxious to get this into my father's hands. Maybe he'll want to try it out right away. I open the gate that leads to the house.

"All right, let's do it. My mother and sisters are inside. I haven't told them anything about this."

"Did you tell them you were bringing me?"

"No." We're inside the wall that separates my home from the street. "But I think my mother is going to really like finding out my friend Rahim is another boy like me."

Rahim takes a deep breath and straightens his Wizards cap.

"Hope so. If not, I've got a plan."

"What's your plan?"

He touches the rim of his cap and shows me a cunning grin.

"I haven't told you this, but I can do some pretty special things with my lucky magician's hat. If things don't look good, I'll just make myself disappear."

I roll my eyes, but I kind of believe what he's telling me. There's always a small truth to what Rahim says, even if it sounds too wild to be true.

We walk into the everything room. My mother is sitting on a floor cushion. She's got her back against the wall. Her knitting needles are crossing and uncrossing.

"Madar?" I'm holding my surprise behind my back. "I brought a friend home. This is Rahim."

My mother puts down her knitting. She's been making sweaters for my cousins. It seems kind of silly to me since it's the end of winter, but I know she's trying to find a way to pay my uncle and aunt back for all the food and stuff they've brought us in the cold months.

"*Salaam*," Rahim says loudly. He's put on his polite face to greet my mother.

"Hello to you too."

My mother looks from him to me. I know she's

wondering how I could have brought a strange boy, an almost teenager, into our home with my sisters around. It's one thing for me to play with the boys in the neighborhood but pretty inappropriate to bring a boy into the privacy of our home since I've got three sisters to think of.

"Obayd, why don't you boys play outside? Your sisters are in the back hanging up the laundry and . . ."

Before I can open my mouth to say anything, the expression on my mother's face changes.

"Oh."

She sees Rahim for what he is. Or, more important, for what he's not. She breathes a sigh of relief.

"For a second, I thought you had . . ." She shakes her head. "Never mind. What are you boys up to?"

"I've got something for Father. We made something for him."

"*You* made it. I was just there," Rahim says.

I stand a little taller, hearing him say that.

"What is it?" my mother asks.

I set the walking stick in front of me. Her eyebrows go up.

"You made this for your father? How?" She is curious enough that she's on her feet. Rahim and I shoot each other proud looks as she touches the ledge, pinches it between her fingers, and steps back to admire our work. "Boys, this looks wonderful!"

"Do you think he'll like it?"

She purses her lips together.

"He should. He really should. It's a very thoughtful thing to do for him." She laughs. "And I thought all you did was play games and look for ways to get dirty."

"We can do much more than that!" Rahim says with a grin.

"You certainly can. And do you know why? Do you know what's special about the two of you?" my mother asks softly. "You are the best of both worlds—one half from the east and one half from the west."

Rahim and I are not quite sure what she means by that, but it sounds like a good thing to me. I think I notice her eyes get a little moist, but before I can be sure she takes a deep breath and puts her hands on her hips.

"What are you waiting for? Go on and take it in to him."

Rahim hangs back when I walk toward the bedroom. My mother nudges him forward.

"It's okay, dear. You can go with him. He should thank you both for the work you've put into this."

We stand in the doorway. My father is resting on his side, his back to us. Rahim looks a little uncomfortable but mostly excited. We've been imagining this moment since the day we spotted the grumpy old man in the market.

"Padar?" I call out softly. When he doesn't answer I

turn and whisper to Rahim. "He doesn't hear very well because of the explosion."

Rahim nods in understanding.

"Padar," I say loudly. "I've got my friend here with me. We've got something for you."

My father rolls onto his back. It's a huge effort.

"My boy, I'm resting," he says flatly. "Another time."

"But, Padar, we've worked so hard on this. I think you're going to like it. Please look, Father!"

I can already picture him standing with it, running his fingers down the stick and laughing, like my mother did, at how we must have made this fine crutch. He turns his head in our direction. His eyelids look heavy.

"What is it?"

"It's a walking stick. We made it ourselves. I climbed a tree to get the stick and then we got some cardboard and folded it up and cut these parts out so it fits right here. Do you want to try it? We didn't measure it exactly, but I think it's the right height for you. Please try it, Padar-*jan*!"

"A walking stick?"

"Yes!"

My father lets his head fall against the pillow. He takes a deep breath.

"Just go."

I think, for a second, that I've heard him wrong. I look at Rahim, but his eyes are on the ground.

"But, Padar, I think if you just try it . . . We saw a guy . . ."

My father's eyes are closed tight, like he's trying to squash the storm that's rising in his chest. It doesn't work. He props himself up on his elbows and his words explode into our silent little home.

"Did you bring your friend here to shame me? You want him to see your broken father? You want to put me on display like an animal? Where's your respect for your father? That's what I need from you, not some stupid walking stick!"

My stomach drops.

"Get out!" the storm continues. "Get out, get out, get out, both of you! You boys think you're men? You think you know what it is to be a man? You don't know a single thing about it, you weak little freaks . . ."

My mother is by my side.

"Enough!" she thunders. Her arms are on my shoulders. "That's enough shouting. You haven't eaten. It's doing nothing for your pain to go hungry. Let me fix you something and we can leave the walking stick for another time."

"I need to be left alone. Out, out, out, all of you!" He flops back onto the flat floor cushion with a sad groan. He's run out of fuel.

I take a step backward. For some reason, I don't step on Rahim's toes. I spin around, my face burning red to have brought my friend into this mess.

Rahim's not there.

My mother turns to look for him too.

There was no puff of smoke. There was no sparkle of lights. There was no twirling cape. There was nothing dazzling or spectacular about it, but it was as close to real magic as I have ever seen. I'd had my back to him for just a moment, blown over by my father's rant. I look around, but there's not a trace of Rahim, not even the sound of footsteps or the slamming of the metal gate outside of our house.

Sixteen

Yesterday was the first day of spring, which is Nowruz. It's the first day of the year and always comes with a lot of excitement. When we lived in Kabul, Nowruz meant coloring hard-boiled eggs, eating white rice with seasoned spinach, and getting lots of sweets and even some money from the adults. I was looking forward to it again this year, but it ended up not being as festive as I hoped. My uncle asked us to come over, but my father didn't feel up to going, and my mother didn't want to leave him alone, so we stayed home.

We boiled some eggs but didn't bother to color them, deciding to play our egg-fighting game behind the house. My sisters and I tapped our eggs against one another's to see whose would break first. I thought I might win this year, as if my egg would somehow be stronger than theirs in my boy hands. It doesn't seem to work that way, though. My shell was shattered by Neela's egg, and both Neela's and Meena's eggs surrendered to Alia's. She was so happy that she almost forgot all the other fun Nowruz activities we were missing out on.

Today, the day after Nowruz, is the first day of school and it is starting to drizzle. Not enough that they will call us in from recess but just enough to settle the dust on the playground. The other boys have splintered off into small groups. Most of the girls are huddled under an awning. Rahim showed up today in a very unmagical way. He walked onto the schoolyard as if what happened in my home last week was something I imagined. But I can't *not* say something about it.

"I didn't know he was going to be so upset. Sorry it was like that."

"Don't worry about it."

"He was having a bad day, I guess." I don't know how else to explain what he saw. Rahim takes off his Wizards hat and runs his fingers through his shaggy hair.

"You want to know something? My father has pretty bad days too."

"He does?"

Rahim nods. This is the first time he's said anything

about his father, and I'm curious what he's like, especially compared to mine.

"But, Rahim, my father called us freaks."

"No one's called me anything like that," Rahim says. "But maybe he's right. Maybe we *are* freaks."

"Isn't there anything you miss about being a girl?"

"Nothing," Rahim says. "You?"

I shrug.

"I guess I miss my hair sometimes."

Rahim bites his lip and touches the back of his neck.

"I had really long hair," he whispers. "It reached the middle of my back and was a little curly. Kind of like Neela's hair."

"I used to get all my sisters' clothes. Meena's got this one dress now that's getting small on her. It's purple and pink with silver embroidery on the front and on the hem. Our neighbor in Kabul gave it to us as a gift. I've been waiting for my turn to wear it, and now that it's my size, I don't wear dresses."

"Purple used to be my favorite color."

"I bet purple would look good on you," I tell Rahim.

"I bet that dress would look really nice on you," he tells me. "Too bad no one makes really pretty pants, huh?"

I laugh, picturing my blue corduroys with pink and purple embroidery on them.

"That's the problem with being half things," Rahim

admits. "It's hard if you think you're missing something. I don't want to be a half thing. I just want to be one whole normal me."

So do I.

"Do you know what I heard last week? I heard there's a boy like us who is a grown man—as old as our fathers."

I shake my head. That cannot be true. I know how Rahim feels about the idea of being turned back into a girl. Maybe he's making this up because he wants it to be true.

"That's impossible. No one is going to let a teenage girl hang around with teenage boys. What parents would let their daughter embarrass them like that?"

Rahim is convinced.

"Actually, my great-great-grandmother was like us too. She dressed as a man and worked as a guard for a king."

"A king? King of what?"

"King of Afghanistan, you donkey!"

I'm pretty sure Rahim is making this up, but I don't feel like arguing today. Rahim's spine straightens. His right hand goes up like he's stopping traffic. He's got something serious he wants to talk about.

"You like this, don't you? Life as a boy is good."

I have spent five months and three days as a boy. My ears don't seem as big anymore. My arms are stronger. I like the way the sun hits my face when I run. I have knocked out other players in *ghursai*. A lot of days my father smiles when I come running home, my pants brown and worn at the knees, my hair matted with sweat. The teacher doesn't call me to the front of the classroom anymore because she knows I can solve the equations and, more important, that I will not turn white with my classmates staring at my back. I can climb trees and hang upside down, letting the blood rush to my head.

To my cousins, my neighbors, my aunts and uncles, I am Obayd. I want to be nothing else.

"Of course, Rahim. Why are you even asking? What else is there to be?"

Rahim doesn't look at me. He kicks at the ground.

"There's nothing else to be. Not for me. I only want to be what I am now."

"Honestly, Rahim. I can't picture you as anything else."

My comment makes him happy. I wonder if he's talking about this stuff because of what my mother said—about us being one half from the east and one half from the west. I really didn't think she meant anything bad by it.

"Neither can I. But I don't know if everyone would agree with us. Other boys like us have to change. I've heard it's bad."

"What do you mean?"

"They say we're not supposed to stay like this forever. They say we're supposed to be girls again. Before we get too old. I heard my mother talking to my aunt about it.

My mother said she's heard some boys like us don't know what to do when they're changed back. They get confused and act really weird. I don't like the sound of that, so I've been thinking about it, and last night I had an idea."

"I'm not confused, and I don't think you are either," I snap at him, ignoring the fact that he had an idea. I wish he hadn't brought up what might happen when kids like us are changed back.

But we both turn quiet, wondering if I'm right or if we would even be able to see this in ourselves. I don't think my head is scrambled. And, although he may be a bit smug at times, I'm pretty sure Rahim's head is fine too. We've spent mornings, afternoons, and evenings together, believing that what we are is the most normal thing there is. We know we're smarter than the boys and stronger than the girls. It's not something we say in words. It's something we say in the way we pat each other on the back or laugh when one of the boys fumbles playing soccer. It's in the look Rahim shoots me when we run past a group of girls trying to keep the wind from blowing their head scarves away. It's in the way we take our time going home after school, knowing we don't have to rush. While boys play in one courtyard and girls play in another, Rahim and I skip along the imaginary high wall that divides them, closer to the sky than anyone else. We are untouchable.

"I don't feel messed up at all," Rahim says confidently. "But I can promise you this—if someone tries to tell me I'm a girl, I'll be so angry that I'll mess *him* up in the head."

And that's why I love Rahim.

"I'd like to see that!"

"Consider yourself invited, my friend."

I start to wonder how we wound up here, Rahim inviting me to the match between my best friend and the imaginary person who dares to call him a girl (even though he is one). When I remember, I become curious.

"Wait, you said you had an idea. What was it?"

Rahim juts his chin out and beams.

"You want to know, don't you?"

"Sure, why not?"

"I remember my mother telling us about a legend once—about Rostam's bow. The legend says that passing under a rainbow changes boys to girls and girls to boys. Even if a pregnant woman walks under the rainbow, the baby in her belly changes."

This sounds vaguely familiar. I bet my grandparents told me this story when I was little.

"I think we should do it," Rahim whispers.

"Do what? Pass under a rainbow?"

"It's easier than passing over one."

"You're serious."

"I am. I want to go under the rainbow and be changed

forever. I don't want this to be temporary. Do you?"

"Of course not . . . You know that. But is it just a story or is true? Do you know anyone who's been changed by going under a rainbow?"

Rahim shakes his head.

"No. But I think it's true. Everyone knows the story. My mom and aunt heard it from their grandparents. Imagine how long ago their grandparents must have first learned about it—at least a hundred years ago. If it weren't true, people wouldn't still be talking about it. There are probably people we know who have done it but aren't saying a thing about it. It's not like you can tell by looking at a person."

"I don't know. What made you come up with this idea?"

Rahim looks at the ground.

"I have this feeling . . . like something's going to happen. My mother saw me playing in the street yesterday with the guys. We were just messing around, doing some karate moves, play wrestling. It wasn't a big deal, just normal stuff. But my mother had this look on her face like I was running through the streets naked or something. She wouldn't even talk to me when I went home."

"You think she's going to change you back." I understand now why Rahim is digging up legends and looking for ways to save himself from being undone. My friend might talk tough, but at the end of the day, we both know we're not in charge once we walk through our front doors and back into our homes. Everything changes then. We go from being kings of our own fates to children ruled by parents. And parents have good days and bad days, or moments when they're not sure if they're doing the right thing. Those doorways, they're the opposite of a rainbow. They're thick black nets across a blue sky.

Rahim feels it now. His mother is looking at him differently. He needs to act before she does.

I hear the slow roll of thunder in the distance. The sky has darkened without my noticing. Rahim takes a deep breath. Each drop of moisture catches a speck of dust, making the air just a little bit softer going through our lungs.

The raindrops are fatter, heavy enough that I feel each drop as it hits my head, a tiny, cold tickle on my scalp before it slides down the back of my neck. Across the yard, I spy one girl as she peeks out from under the awning. She reaches her right hand out, palm up. She takes a step away from the shelter and into the yard, both palms to the sky. She turns her face upward and lets the rain fall on her cheeks, her eyelids, her lips. She sticks out the very tip of her tongue and her nose crinkles playfully. She looks incredibly happy, as if a few silly drops of rain might be the very best thing that's ever happened to her.

In that moment, I'm convinced. It's time for us to chase down a rainbow.

Seventeen

I can tell my sisters are awake when I hear them moving, coughing, or talking. With my father, it's the opposite. He rarely makes a sound when he's awake, but that's not true when he's sleeping. When his eyes are closed, his breathing turns into a rough, raspy snore. I bet our neighbor can count his breaths, since the courtyards outside our homes are separated only by the thin clay wall. She probably does, too. She's really nosy. That's her thing.

I stand in the hallway knowing my father must be awake because all is quiet—I don't even hear the sound of normal breathing. I picture him on his mattress, staring at the ceiling or at the family picture hung up on the wall. I inch closer to the doorway and peek in. My father is lying on his side. His eyes are closed, but there's no snoring.

"Padar?" I whisper. I tread carefully, afraid of another outburst.

His eyelids open as if he'd been waiting for me to speak. "Yes, my son."

I can tell he's not upset with me today. Relieved, I step into the room and sit in a wooden chair with a fabric seat. My mother sits in this chair when she wants to talk to my father. My sisters and I pretend not to hear her begging him to come to the everything room or to let some of his cousins drop by for a visit. The walking stick I made is in the corner of the room, against the wall. I'm sure my mother put it there. I turn away. Looking at it is like going back to that day.

"Padar, how are you?" My father's eyes lighten softly. "How is your pain?"

"I'm fine, Obayd. Hearing you talk makes me feel better. How is school?"

I hear my Kabul father, not my angry, one-legged father. I can breathe.

"Good. My teacher says my handwriting is much better than it was just a few months ago. She even asked if I spent the winter months practicing. And I got a really good score on the first science test to see what we remembered from before winter break."

"Science, eh? That's good. I never had a head for science.

Still, I wanted to be a doctor. Did I ever tell you that? I wanted to walk through a hospital and have sick people feel happy to see me."

"You would have been a good doctor, Padar-*jan*."

"Maybe. Too bad we only get one life."

I've stared at the picture behind me for hours. It's etched into my memory in painful detail. The photograph was taken while we lived in Kabul and in the picture there are six of us—my parents and their four girls. My father and mother are sitting on a love seat, with straight faces and straighter backs. My father is wearing an olive-colored suit and he has a neat little mustache. My mother is wearing a black dress with faint gray flowers across the collar. She has on a light gray head scarf just behind her bangs, which are brushed to the side and tucked behind her ear. She has small emerald earrings that she sold before we left Kabul. Neela and Meena are standing on either side of my parents in floral-print dresses. Alia and I are kneeling in front in our matching violet sweaters and indigo skirts.

In the photograph, I'm kneeling right in front of my father, hiding his two perfect legs from view. I wish I could move myself in the picture so we could at least have an image of my father with two legs. That way we wouldn't always imagine him the way he looks now. I wonder if my father stares at this photograph thinking the same thing and wishing he could just nudge me to the side.

"You were a good police officer."

"What do you want to be, Obayd?" It's an unusual question for my father to ask, and I'm not sure how to answer. All I've been able to think of lately is what I *don't* want to be.

"Maybe I'll be an engineer. Definitely not a farmer. If it were up to me to water your pepper plants, they would have died a long time ago."

He laughs. It's a sound I rarely hear, and I'm glad I teased it out of him. It feels like the biggest thing I've done in weeks. The room becomes silent again. I hesitate to talk, not wanting to ruin the moment.

"What have you been learning in school?"

"Lots of different things. We've been looking at maps, learning the names of mountains . . ."

"When I was your age, I spent my days wandering all over this village with my brothers. We could have used a map."

I cannot imagine my father ever having been my age. I wonder if we would have been friends.

"Did you ever find anything?"

My father takes a deep breath in and lets it out.

"We once went to an old shrine—a place where people pray and tie little ribbons to the fence for good luck. They say if you go there and wish for something, it will come true. My brothers and I ripped off strips of cloth from the hems of our pants since we didn't have anything else with us. Your grandmother was so angry . . ."

I burst into laughter. My father smiles.

"What did you wish for?" I ask.

"If you asked any kid in the village what he wanted, he would tell you the same thing—a bicycle. That's what I wished for too."

"And did you get it?"

"The bicycle? Believe it or not, your grandfather came home with a bicycle one week later. Not just for me, of course. It was for all of us. But I got my turn on it too."

I think of what Rahim and I would do with a bicycle. I picture him pedaling and me riding on the bar in front. We would zip through town, teasing the other boys as we passed them and knocking their hats off so fast they wouldn't know what had happened. We'd whiz past girls who could never dream of being allowed to ride a bike.

"Where is the shrine?"

"Doesn't exist anymore. It was destroyed in the war," my father says. He picks up a glass of water and takes a sip.

"Where else did you go?"

"A lake once. Oh, but the best place we ever found was a waterfall."

I can hear my sisters laughing in the kitchen.

"Where was that? I've never seen a waterfall."

"We stumbled onto it. That's what happens when you have nothing better to do and a few older brothers to lead the way. We walked for a few hours to get there. Walked, climbed, and crawled, actually. We found a foot path on the edge of the village where the mountains run. We were boys and doing things we shouldn't have been doing, as usual. I remember hearing this sound, like a wet roar, that got louder and louder the farther we walked. We didn't know what it was, but we had to find out."

"That loud? Was it the waterfall?"

"It was. If we could have, we would have climbed to the top to see where the water was coming from, but it was too rocky even for a bunch of headstrong boys like us." My father stares off, as if he can see it all in front of him again. "I'll never forget that place. We stood at the bottom and stared up. The water was coming down with such force. The mist and the rainbows and the air . . ."

I don't hear a thing my father says after that.

Rainbows.

"Padar-*jan*," I exclaim, as I stand up in a burst. The chair nearly falls over. My father looks at me quizzically. "I just remembered something I've got to do for school tomorrow . . . homework . . . and if I don't do it . . . I'll come back in a little bit . . ."

I'm walking backward and miss the doorway, knocking

the back of my head on the wall. I spin into the hallway and feel my heart pounding. I need to get to Rahim.

I run straight into the courtyard and stumble into my mother as she enters the gate. My mother's hands fly up and across her belly. She's wearing a navy blue house dress with a sash at the waist. My mouth drops open. I see a roundness I haven't seen before. My mother looks at my face and starts to explain, but she doesn't have to. I suddenly understand that my mother's loose dresses have been hiding something—she's pregnant.

"Obayd-*jan*, I suppose it's time to share the news . . ." she says hesitantly.

"Madar-*jan*, your belly is . . ."

"This is good news for our family. We're going to have a new baby soon."

"A baby. Mother, you . . ."

Her eyes sparkle with a flash of hope.

"I didn't want to say anything yet, but it's not something I can hide much longer."

If it's a girl, she'll be in line to wear some hand-me-downs. Maybe they'll make her a *bacha posh* since she'll be younger and easier to disguise.

Then again, maybe it's a boy. If it is a boy, I'm finished. My parents will have the son they need and my work as a *bacha posh* will be complete. I have a knot in my stomach, the same one Rahim's got.

My mother sees the disappointment on my face. She bites her lip.

"Obayd," she calls out. But I'm already out the gate, my sandals pounding against the street and tears streaming down my face. I've got to get to Rahim. There's a clock ticking for both of us, and I might just have found our solution.

I know where to find rainbows that don't run away.

Eighteen

Rahim and I have been trying to figure out how we're going to get under a rainbow. We've come across a few problems.

First of all, it rains only about once a month in our village.

We did actually spot rainbows twice since we started looking—once on the far end of a pond and another time behind our school. We were feeling pretty gutsy and went after them, but it was useless. As much as we ran, the rainbow was never any closer. It might as well have been on the moon.

That's why I'm excited to tell Rahim my idea.

"A waterfall," I announce with a sly grin. I am early

for school and find him in the yard, leaning against a tree. He's trying to finish a homework assignment before classes start and is too distracted to hear me.

"Rahim, are you listening? A waterfall. That's what we need."

"Yeah, yeah, I'm listening. A waterfall. What are you talking about?"

When I tell Rahim about the waterfall, he puts down his pencil. He's not excited, but there's urgency in his voice.

"We'll leave right after we're dismissed," he plans. "We can't waste any time."

I walk into my classroom feeling like there's something my friend is not sharing with me.

We set out right after school. There are four mountains that separate our village from the province on the other side. I stare at the slopes, my hand over my eyes to block the bright sun.

"Which one do you think it is?" Rahim asks.

"My father said it was so big that he couldn't climb to the top. He said it was loud enough that they could hear it way before they reached it."

We are walking through an open, dusty plain. There are patches of tall, yellow-green grasses along the way but not much else. There isn't much water around here, and plants don't survive.

We walk really carefully and keep our eyes on the ground. We don't want anything slithering out from under the rocks and catching us by surprise. There are snakes and scorpions in these parts, and we all learn to watch out for them. They're poisonous and sometimes deadly. I don't want to lose my leg. I feel bad thinking it, but I don't want to end up like my father.

I try to retrace my father's childhood footsteps. Which way would he have gone? The mountain range runs along the eastern edge of our village. In the mornings, you can see the sun rise up from behind the peaks. Kabul is on the other side of those mountains. Not right on the other side, but a few days' travel. There are spots of green on the mountainside where trees have managed to take root.

"How are we ever going to find the waterfall?" Rahim wonders out loud.

Looking at the peaks in front of me, I'm thinking the same thing.

We walk on, glancing over our shoulders every few minutes and hoping we'll be able to find our way back.

"You see those trees over there? There are five of them together in a bunch. There might be a trail to the left of them, between those two mountains. Maybe that's the path your father took. Did he tell you anything else about how they found the waterfall?"

"No, he didn't, but I think that might be it," I say

hopefully. "He said there was a footpath. And if there are trees, there might be water, right?"

We're reassured by our bit of science and decide to go for the path we've spotted. We walk for an hour. We're too worried to talk much. I've made a list in my head of what could go wrong: we might have picked the wrong path, we might not find our way home, and the waterfall might not be there anymore. It's not a very encouraging list.

"How much farther do you think it is?" Rahim is getting impatient.

"I don't know," I mumble. "I thought we would have been there already."

I almost feel like the mountain is moving away from us. We don't seem to be getting any closer, and we've been walking for nearly two hours. Thankfully, it is spring and the days are getting longer again. The sun warms us. Even though it's not that hot outside, we've been walking for a while and my shirt sticks to my skin.

"You're not wearing your Wizards hat," I say, noticing.

"Yeah, wrong day to forget my hat," Rahim says. "You know, I got it right after I changed. I wear it almost every day."

I know by "changed," my friend means when he became a boy.

"I didn't believe you at first but I know it really is a

lucky hat. Because the way you were acting when I first met you, you're lucky I agreed to be your friend!"

Rahim gives me a playful shove. "Sometimes you can be pretty funny, Obayd. *Sometimes.*"

We reach the footpath at sunset. Our stomachs are growling; our legs are achy. Our sandals are cheap plastic things that don't do much for a rocky walk like this. I can already feel the blisters bubbling.

"I'm thirsty." I only mean to say it, but it comes out as a whine.

"I am too," Rahim agrees. "When we get to the waterfall, there'll be plenty to drink."

If *we get to the waterfall.*

We start along the trail, a little nervous to be this far from home. The sky is more purple than blue now, and it's completely quiet.

"Are you sure about this?" I ask Rahim.

"It's got to be close. It just has to," he insists, but I'm not sure. I know that being sure is his thing, even when he's not right. "Do you hear any water?"

We both stop walking and listen really carefully for the wet roar my father told me about.

Shhhh.

I put my hands on my hips. I wasn't making a sound and don't appreciate Rahim shushing me.

"You're the one making noise," I whisper. "Tell yourself to shush."

Shhhh.

"Obayd, that wasn't me," Rahim whispers back.

We're both frozen in place. My heart starts to pound, and I feel my palms get sweaty. We hear it again. I'm looking at the ground around me. Rahim's doing the same. There are big rocks on either side of the trail and smaller rocks everywhere. It's starting to get dark enough that it's hard to see in the shadows.

I'm about to say we should leave when I feel a tickle on my ankle. It feels like a leather belt, sliding against my foot. I'm already tense because it's dark and we hear something and there's no food in my belly to settle my nerves.

My leg reacts with lightning speed, kicking into the air to get whatever it is as far away from me as possible. It takes my brain a second to realize what happened. When it registers, my scream breaks the evening quiet.

"Snaaaake!"

Rahim grabs my hand.

"Is it on you? Did it bite you?"

"No, no, but I felt it! I kicked it off!"

"Where is it?"

"I don't know. Maybe over there somewhere!"

We are more silent than we've ever been. I don't hear anything.

A shiver runs down my spine.

"I want to go back."

"We're so close," Rahim says. "The waterfall could be just on the other side of this hill."

"Or it could be on another mountain," I whisper. It's like we've decided, without talking about it, that whispering is smarter than speaking out loud. "We can't see where we're going, and we're hungry. We're not going to make it very far."

"We've come all this way." Rahim sounds really disappointed. "We need to be brave."

This makes me angry. Easy for Rahim to say we should be brave when he's not the one who had a snake on his foot.

"I *am* brave," I say sharply. "I'm just not stupid."

"If you didn't want to come here, you should have said so. I could have come on my own."

"Rahim, I'm the one who had the idea to find this waterfall, remember? Don't be like that. Let's come back another day—in the morning, so we can see where we're going."

Rahim stares at the ground. His shoulders are slumped. I try to touch him, but he pulls back sharply—like I'm the snake.

"Fine. You do whatever you want, but I'm going back."

I say it, but neither of us budges. The truth is we're

both just as scared of moving as we are of staying in one place. Being trapped by something we can't see is an awful feeling.

Rahim takes a couple of big breaths.

"Fine," he says with defeat. "We'll go back."

We turn around. We don't talk at all. I'm pretty annoyed with Rahim for telling me I should be brave. That's the same thing as calling me a coward, which I'm not. He's not acting like himself, and I don't know why.

"I can't believe you kicked that snake off you. That was pretty brave, Obayd."

"Thanks," I say like it was no big deal. Rahim is still quiet, but at least we're not mad at each other anymore.

"Hey, Rahim," I say. I really want to change his mood. "Maybe we can try again on Friday when there's no school? We can leave really early in the morning so we have plenty of time to get here. And I'll see if my dad remembers anything else about the waterfall. Maybe I can get a better idea of which way to go."

Rahim is a few steps ahead of me.

"Yeah, that's probably a good idea," he says. "Maybe today wasn't meant to be the day we find the waterfall."

"What do you mean?"

"You know, destiny and fate and all that."

"Do you believe in that destiny stuff?"

Rahim slows his step and lets me catch up. We are

walking side by side, our elbows bumping against each other in the darkness. It's not annoying, though. It feels like an arm around my shoulders. Rahim gives my question about fate some thought before answering.

"Sometimes I do and sometimes I don't. I guess if something good happens to me, I'd rather not believe destiny had anything to do with it. I'd rather believe it was something I did."

"And what if something bad happens to you? Then would you believe in destiny?"

Rahim's voice turns cold and hard.

"Then I'd wish destiny was a person so I could kick him in the face."

Nineteen

At the schoolyard, I wait for Rahim. It is early, and he should be here soon. I see Ashraf and Abdullah walking together.

Rahim and I got home late last night, and I wonder if he got into as much trouble as I did. My mother was so furious with me that she refused to unlock the gate and let me in. When I started to apologize to her (which involved pleading at the top of my lungs), she opened the gate really fast, grabbed me by my elbow, and practically threw me into our courtyard.

She said all the things I knew she would say. I'd known I'd get in trouble for coming home so late, but it might have been worth it if we'd actually made it to the waterfall or a rainbow. It also occurred to me that even if we had made it to the waterfall, the sky had already gone from oranges and violets to dark blues and grays. There wasn't enough light to even make a rainbow. I wanted to kick myself for being so dumb.

My mother was so mad that all her thoughts came out in one long string of *Where were you?* and *Are you trying to make me crazy?* and *What was I supposed to think happened to you?* Her voice went from a slow, angry pace to a fast, hurt one. I couldn't argue with her so I kept my head down and mumbled a slow, stream of *I'm really sorry, Mother* and *I promise I'll never do it again.*

We never actually did talk about where I had gone or why.

School starts and Rahim is still not here. I sit through classes, my restless foot tapping out the seconds until recess. I am the first one in the yard. I search through the groups of boys, but there is no one wearing a blue Wizards hat.

Rahim is not there.

"Hey, Ashraf . . . Abdullah," I call out. Ashraf turns around. He's toeing a soccer ball and is about to pass it to Abdullah when I interrupt.

"Little guy," he says with a nod. "What's up?"

Ashraf and Abdullah treat me like there are way more than three years between us. But they don't tease me too much more than that, so I don't complain. Abdullah takes a step closer.

"Have you guys seen Rahim?"

They shake their heads. Rahim was not in class today.

"We got home late last night, and I wanted to see if he got in trouble. I sure did."

The boys chuckle.

"What were you doing out so late?"

"Oh . . . we were just . . ." I look at the ball under Ashraf's foot. "We were playing soccer."

"That late?"

"Yeah, we do that sometimes."

Abdullah looks at me like he senses something's up. I leave Rahim's friends and join up with a couple of boys from my own class. They're playing a game of tag. My legs are still sore from yesterday's hike, so they catch me right away. And I'm too tired to catch them back.

Three more days go by. Then the weekend. A new school week starts and Rahim is nowhere to be found.

"Still nothing?" Abdullah asks. We're all pretty concerned at this point.

"I bet I know what happened," Ashraf says. We wait for his theory. "I bet his mother and father were upset that he came home late that night. I think they're keeping him home as punishment."

"Not even letting him go to school?" I ask. That's the part that doesn't make sense to me.

"Sure," Ashraf says. "I've heard his father is kind of rough."

"What do you mean?" I feel uncomfortable. Why don't I know anything about Rahim's father?

"You know he was in the war. And I hear he's a drug addict—a pretty bad one." Ashraf tells us this in a half whisper, which is the nicer way to say something like that about a friend's father.

"Where'd you hear that?" Abdullah asks.

"From my father. Rahim's father still goes off and fights sometimes with the warlord Abdul Khaliq. And I know some people have seen him going up and down their street. He talks to himself. He stumbles around and he can't even answer a simple *How are you?* most days."

How could Rahim's father be such a brute and Rahim not even mention this to me once? I am feeling like my best friend is a stranger to me. I realize I know he has a mother, father, and four sisters. I've heard him mention his aunt, the one with the hunchback, who came up with the idea to change Rahim into a *bacha posh*. Other than that, I don't know much about his life away from school.

"That bad, huh?" Abdullah shakes his head.

"That bad." We all know people addicted to opium. People use it to relax or kill the pain and then they get addicted and can't let it go. I know because my father told us about it. He swore to my mother that he would never be hooked the way he'd seen some people get hooked. He told us about the people begging and dying for opium. He said he'd ask God to help him manage, since we can't afford to keep him numb with pills.

I feel really bad for Rahim. And I think I'm better off with a one-legged father than an opium-addicted one. It occurs to me that it's a really weird thing to think and I should probably never say it out loud.

I make up my mind to stop by his home after school this week if he doesn't come back. I know where he lives though I've never been inside. When Rahim doesn't show up for the next two days, I stick with my plan. I follow the path he's shown me and find the bright green door, metal rusting on the edges. I consider knocking but am too afraid Rahim's father will answer. I stand there feeling foolish and wondering if my friend is just a few feet away from me. I listen closely. What am I expecting to hear? Yelling? Crying? Laughing? I cannot imagine.

I turn my back to the door. If I'm not going to knock, I should just leave. I hesitate because I know if the tables were turned, Rahim would knock on my door. My best friend wouldn't be so scared. I bet he would—

I hear the footsteps too late to move away.

The door creaks open and a hand clamps down on my shoulder.

Twenty

"Who are you?"

She is suspicious and has a right to be, I suppose. I feel my heart race.

"Uh, I'm a friend of Rahim."

She closes her eyes for a second too long—it gives me a bad feeling.

"What are you doing here?"

Rahim told me about his sisters. I know their names and a little about their personalities. This girl's voice is even and mature. I think I know who she is.

"My name is Obayd. Are you his sister? Are you Shahla?"

I can tell by the look on her face that the answer is yes.

"Please, I just want to see him. Is he home?" My nerves are settling a little. Shahla is Rahim's oldest sister. She should be in Neela's class, but Rahim's father doesn't let his daughters go to school. I remember Rahim telling me this months ago, just before winter break started. He had his hands balled up in fists when he talked about it, and it wasn't because it was cold outside.

"You can't see Rahima—I mean, Rahim. You can't see him."

"What's happened to him? When is he coming back to school?"

I can hear voices inside. A man is yelling.

"Shahla! Who's at the door? Get back in here." It must be Rahim's father. I remember what Abdullah and Ashraf told me about him and imagine a beast of a man stumbling around the house in a rage. I imagine a gun slung over his shoulder.

I might throw up.

"I'm coming, Padar. It's just one of the children from the neighborhood," Shahla calls out quickly.

Shahla looks back at me and blinks rapidly. I can see her eyes water.

"You should just go home. You're only going to get yourself into a lot of trouble if you stick around here." She takes a step back into their courtyard and makes a move to close their front door. She's saying what I've already been thinking. I've wanted to leave Rahim's house ever since I first came here. The shouting has stopped, but I'm pretty sure something bad is going on inside their home. My shoulders sag.

Run away, a voice inside my head tells me.

I want to, I think, *but I still don't know what's happened to Rahim.*

What was it that my best friend had told me when we first met?

You stand like you're not sure you should be here. Are you supposed to be here, Obayd?

I am. My back straightens.

I lodge my foot against the bottom of the door to stop Shahla from closing it on me. She looks up with surprise and shakes her head. She leans in and makes her voice a whisper. "Look, I'm only trying to help you. Go home and forget about Rahim."

"I can't forget about him. He's my best friend!"

That's the truth. He's the one who made everything okay. I would've been lost without him, fumbling through school confused about what I was supposed to do or be. Rahim showed me that being a *bacha posh* is a good thing, maybe even the greatest thing that's ever happened to me.

"Obayd," Shahla says with a sigh. "You're just like him."

I like that she thinks so.

"You better watch out for yourself. Boys like you and

Rahima are not boys forever. From what I can see, it's even worse that way. You can wear pants and act like you're going to knock this door down, but you're still a girl. You can't escape that."

"Why do you keep calling him Rahima? He's Rahim." I don't like that Shahla's talking about me being a girl. I am sure Rahim wouldn't stand for it. "I'm not leaving until I see Rahim."

"You can't see Rahima."

The door is flung wide-open, and Shahla is shoved aside. Suddenly, I'm staring at a beast of a man. His clothes are wrinkled and his small, beady eyes and unshaven face look downright menacing. Abdullah and Ashraf were so right about Rahim's father.

"Who are you? What do you want?" he roars.

I take a deep breath. Shahla is standing behind her father. Her eyes go wide and she points with her eyeballs. Just like the dancing I used to do to Indian music, the message comes through the eyes. She's telling me to leave.

If I weren't afraid it would make my situation worse, I would definitely throw up.

"*Salaam,*" I manage to get out. I'm hoping some good manners might soften him up. "*Salaam,* sir. I am a friend of Rahim, and I just came to visit since he hasn't been to school in a few days."

"Get out of here. Rahima's not going back to school, and

she's not coming out to play. Time for you to find some new friends, little boy." His eyes are bloodshot and his words sound a little garbled. He's standing with his feet wide apart, like he might lose his balance if he's not careful.

He's a drug addict, Ashraf had said about Rahim's father. *He talks to himself. He stumbles around and he can't even answer a* How are you? *most days.*

I've never seen anyone act like this, and it makes me extra nervous. I try to peek around him, still hoping to catch a glimpse of Rahim, but the man in front of me is big enough that I can only see half of Shahla.

"Rahima's engaged to be married, and she needs to act like a respectable girl. Enough of this nonsense. This house has been out of control for too long. Now get out of here and don't come back!"

Married? My stomach drops. I must have heard him wrong. Rahim is barely thirteen years old. He can't be getting married!

"You don't hear me, eh?" He takes a step toward me. "What's your father's name? Who's raised such a disobedient mule of a child? Let me tell your father that his son's been chasing after the warlord's bride. I doubt you'll be allowed out of the house when he hears that!"

I can hear Ashraf's voice in my head again.

Rahim's father still goes off and fights sometimes with the warlord.

I don't want Rahim's father to know my father's name. Our village is small enough that if he asks a couple of people, he'll be led straight to our door, which would take very little effort to knock down. I'm sure now that I'm in over my head.

"I'm . . . I'm really sorry, sir. I should just . . . I didn't mean any disrespect," I stutter.

"What's your father's name?" he thunders again.

Shahla does a quick wave with her hand. *Just leave*, she's telling me.

In a flash, I am gone. My feet pound against the street. I half expect Rahim's father to come chasing after me, but he doesn't. I run as fast as I can for as long as I can. I pass people walking through the streets. I nearly knock down an old man walking with his grandson. I stop only when my chest burns too much to go on.

I walk the rest of the way home while my head spins with thoughts. It's just past sunset. Rahim is Rahima now. My friend is getting married. Everything's gone so wrong. We didn't make it to the waterfall in time. He didn't get to walk under a rainbow, and look what happened.

Outside my own front door, I hesitate. What's going to happen to me? Rahim said he would never be changed back to a girl, and I believed him. My chest feels heavy. I miss my friend.

Meena opens the door. She grabs me by the hand and pulls me toward her.

"There you are! Come inside and wash up. We're putting dinner out now."

I stumble behind her. In the everything room, my mother is spooning rice and spiced lentils onto plates. She looks up quickly.

"Obayd!" She shakes her head. "Where have you been? Honestly, if the sun didn't go down, I doubt you would ever come home. That's the problem with boys."

I stare at her.

"What's wrong with you, Obayd? Get on in and wash your hands and face. You need to eat something before you go to bed."

I can't bring myself to move. I want to share what I've just learned, but I can't bring myself to talk about Rahim as a bride. It's just too shocking. My mother notices.

"Obayd," she says slowly. "Is something wrong? Did something happen?"

"Rahim."

"Rahim. The boy who helped you with the walking stick? Has something happened to him?"

"He's . . . he's not coming to school anymore."

"Why?" My sisters are listening carefully.

"His father. Rahim is going to be a . . . a girl now." My own words sound insane to me.

"Oh, I see." My mother nods. Her voice is gentle and soothing now. She thinks she understands what I'm so upset about. "Obayd, it's natural. Your friend is old enough that it's time for her to be a young woman. That's her family's decision."

"But he's only thirteen! And they're making him—"

"Obayd, let it be. You know perfectly well these are temporary arrangements. When the time is up, it's up. I explained that to you from the beginning. I'm sure they're doing what's best for her."

What's best for her? Getting married at the age of thirteen can't possibly be what's best for her!

I'm about to argue back when I stop myself. My mother is looking at me strangely. I can't help but wonder what she's thinking. Does she think I'm "old enough" too?

It's coming, I realize. What's happened to Rahim is going to happen to me, too.

Twenty-One

"Neela, I need to talk to you."

My eldest sister is hunched over a schoolbook. There's a single dim lamp in the room. To see anything well we have to get close enough that we can feel the heat coming off the bulb.

"I'm studying. Can we talk later?"

"Please, Neela. I need to talk now."

It's been three days since I dropped by Rahim's home. It's been three days since I heard the crazy news that my best friend is going to get married. Nothing's making any more sense now that three days have gone by. It's still insane. Neela can sense the urgency in my voice. She looks up.

"What is it, Obayd?"

Where do I begin?

"You know Rahim."

"Your friend? Sure. What about him?"

"His family is changing him back to a girl. I mean . . . I think they did already."

Neela looks at me.

"I heard. Have you seen Rahim since they changed her back?"

I shake my head.

"It's probably not all bad," Neela says. "Maybe she's happier being a girl. I'm sure her family told her it would only be for a while anyway. It would be really strange if she got to my age and was still a boy."

"But, Neela, it's worse than that. They're not just changing her back." The rest of what I've got to get out is really hard to say. I cringe to think about it. Neela waits for me to speak. "She's getting married."

Neela squints, like she doesn't trust what she's heard or seen.

"What did you say?"

"I said, she's getting married!" I whisper. I don't want my parents to hear me. Neela's the only person I can turn to now.

"Married? Like husband-and-wife married?"

I nod.

"But she's only—"

"Thirteen," I say, finishing her sentence for her. "Can her parents really do that?"

"Wow. I've heard of young girls getting married off, but I've never actually seen it happen—to someone I know, I mean. And not at thirteen years old. That's crazy!"

I'm glad to hear she agrees. In our world, families routinely get together and decide which girls and boys should be married. But that's usually something that happens later. Not while they're still in school.

"Thirteen years old. I guess it really does happen," she whispers. "I would just die. I can't even imagine what that would be like. Why would they do that to her?"

I can see Neela is just as shocked as I am. And that she's got more questions than answers.

"How did you find out?"

"I went to Rahim's house. I talked to her sister and then . . . then her father came out. He's awful, Neela. He scared me pretty bad."

"You shouldn't have gone there. You know what people have been saying about him." She closes her book. Our conversation has shut down her studying for the evening.

"Did Mother say something about changing you back?"

"No, but she looked at me like she was thinking about it. I wish I hadn't told her about Rahim. I think I gave her the idea! I don't want to be a girl, Neela. I just *can't* be a girl again."

"Obayd, you're going to be a girl at some point. You can't go on like this forever."

"Why not? What's the big deal about changing back? We don't need any more girls in the village or in this house."

"Obayd, they're going to change you back. I even heard them talking about it," she admits reluctantly.

"Who was talking about it?" I explode. "When?"

Neela shushes me and looks over my shoulder to see if anyone's coming into our room. It seems my *Let me tell you what you need to do* aunt, Khala Aziza, dropped by for another visit last week. Neela heard her telling my mother it was time for me to go back to being a girl. I hate that she thinks everything's up to her. She's not my mother and shouldn't act like she is.

I'm more convinced now that I've got to do something. I've got to find a way to save Rahim and myself. The only problem is that the one person who could actually help me do something as important as this is not allowed out of her house. I don't even know how much longer she'll be living with her parents. I get a run of chills down my spine at the thought of Rahim being sent away from her family home.

I can't sleep all night. I strain my ears thinking I might

overhear my parents talking about me. I hear nothing but the sound of my father snoring. It's the most reassuring noise I could ever hope for.

Before the sun is fully up, I creep out of bed. I'm careful not to wake my sisters. The sky is a thousand colors all at once, and the street in front of my house is as quiet as it gets.

I walk into the back courtyard. My stomach growls. Being up all night has made me hungrier than usual.

I walk in circles, my lips tight with frustration. I stand with my back to a wall. I reach around behind my back with my right hand and grab the front of my left shoe. With a deep breath, I begin. One hop, then two. The courtyard dust is like talcum powder, and my fingers slip from the rubber. My left foot slaps against the ground. I grunt and try again.

I'm glad Rahim's not here to see me stumble like I did when I first met him.

I hop three steps and try to bat at an imaginary opponent on my right. The movement throws me off balance, and I come apart. Legs and arms go every which way and I'm on my backside. My ankle stings.

"Argh!" What's happened to me? I see a flutter in the window of my parents' room. The white curtain sways just slightly. I can make out my father's shape but not his face.

My face grows hot. I cannot imagine what my one-legged father must be thinking to see his daughter-son try to hop about with half her body tied up behind her back.

Twenty-Two

Husband. Such an ugly word, worse than a curse. I can't believe that word has anything to do with my friend. It's hard to get over this.

I spend my time thinking about what it's like for her. I know my friend, and I know she would hate to be a girl. But to be a wife? I make sure no one sees me when I think about it because it makes me so angry that I either cry or punch something. Every time.

After a week, it hits me.

Abdul Khaliq. The warlord. I'd been so upset thinking about her as a girl and a wife that I hadn't thought about the man she's engaged to.

Abdul Khaliq.

I first heard the warlord's name when we had just moved to this village. My aunt mentioned his name with widened eyes. I think about the black jeeps I saw in the market and the baker's warning to stop gawking. My uncle talked to my father about a cousin who had disappeared days after getting into an argument with a member of Abdul Khaliq's family. I've heard other people talk about Abdul Khaliq too, but only after they look over their shoulders to make sure no one else is listening in. People don't have many nice things to say about the warlord.

I don't really know what warlords do, but I know this man controls our village. He and his men get driven around in jeeps with tinted windows. The men carry guns over their shoulders and look meaner than the strictest teacher or father. We don't see them too often, and that's fine with me. I don't like the way the streets and people get quiet when they're around.

Around them, everyone acts like a scared little girl.

There goes my stomach again, thinking of what Rahima must be feeling.

I'm out the door and into the street.

"Obayd! Where are you going? I need you to . . ."

My mother's voice trails off as I run down the street. I'll get in trouble for leaving like this, but I've got to do something. I race into the village, past the patch of tulips that have bloomed and the canary singing in a cage hanging outside a shop window. There are lots of people around. It's Friday morning, which is the day the men go into town to pray together at the mosque.

All the men.

"Watch where you're going, boy!"

I nearly plow down a man on a bicycle. I don't even stop to apologize.

I stop only when I reach the baker. I'm panting.

"Oh, you?" he says when he looks up and sees me empty-handed. He's pulling long, oval breads out of the clay oven. He taps his wooden paddle and the bread falls onto a metal tray. "Come back when you've got the dough. I don't make bread out of air."

"Mister, I have a question."

"What is it?"

He plops another flatbread onto the tray. A woman, covered head to toe in a brilliant blue shroud, walks toward us. When she nods at him, he picks up a ball of dough and starts to stretch it out.

"Abdul Khaliq. Where is his home?"

The baker freezes. He stares at me.

"What do you care?"

"I want to know where his home is."

"Why? You looking for a job?" he says with a laugh. But not because my question is funny.

"I need to know."

"It's not hard to find him, son. You can find him just as easily as he can find you." He shakes his head and lowers the dough into the oven. "Does your father know that you're looking for Abdul Khaliq?"

"Have you ever seen my father?" I ask the baker boldly. "Has he ever been here to buy the family bread?"

The baker says nothing, but I see respect in his eyes.

"He's not a person a child should seek out."

"It's important," I say quietly but firmly.

He nods. The woman stands next to me. She holds out a few bills and the baker hands her a tray of warm flatbreads. The warm smell of fresh bread fills the tent. She thanks him through the small grid window of her head covering. When she's out of earshot, the baker turns back to me.

"There's a road east of the mosque. Behind the small park. You've seen it?"

I know that road. It's where I climbed the tree to get the branch for my father's walking stick. That road must lead to the compound.

"I don't know what you're doing, but it's a bad idea! Don't go . . ."

I take off, leaving while his voice trails off behind me.

I pass the patch of trees and see the one I climbed. I remember what it felt like to look down from that height.

But I survived.

The road heads in the opposite direction from the mountains and away from my home. There is nothing else on this road, nothing but Abdul Khaliq. I break into a jog, knowing the morning prayers will end soon and Abdul Khaliq will be on his way back to the compound. After ten minutes, I see clay walls rise in the distance. There's a tower inside the compound that rises above, like a periscope coming out of the water. It's taller than anything in town and tells me I've found Abdul Khaliq's home.

I wonder if Rahima is just behind the wall. I run a little faster, not sure what I'm going to do when I get to the door.

I look back. There's a long stretch of empty road behind me. I'm far from the market. No one knows I'm here. I feel a breeze tickle the back of neck and realize I'm sweating.

It's quiet. All I can hear is the soft clap of my sandals hitting the dirt road.

I can't tell if there's someone in the tower. I keep my eyes away from it.

When I reach the walls, there's nothing I can do but touch them. They're too tall to see over. I listen. I hear kids at play and the thump of a foot hitting a soccer ball. Is my best friend playing in there? I hear laughter.

Maybe things aren't as bad as I've thought.

Before I think about it much more, I pound on the door. I put my ear against the metal and try to make out voices. I would know Rahima's voice anywhere.

The door swings open and I'm face-to-face with a boy I've seen at school. He's older than me. I can tell he's surprised to see me.

"Who are you?"

"I'm . . . I'm . . ."

I hadn't thought this through.

"I think my cousin was brought here."

"Cousin? What cousin?"

"Rahim . . . a." It is a tiny sound at the end, but it makes a huge difference.

His eyebrows go up.

"She's your cousin?"

I nod, trying to look convincing.

"I don't think she's supposed to have family coming here to visit her. Did her parents send you?"

"No." I shake my head. "I just wanted to visit her. I didn't get to see her before she left."

"Oh, I get it!" he exclaims. "You want to see what she looks like now! Yeah, I bet you would." He takes a step back and looks over his shoulder. "Let me see if she's . . ."

I turn and look at the road. I'm expecting to see black jeeps coming back to the compound from the mosque any minute now.

"Hey, your cousin is here!"

I turn around and peer past the open door. I see the courtyard, big enough that all the homes on my block could fit in its belly. There's a well in the middle of it and someone's leaning over it, pulling up a bucket. She's wearing a blue dress and has on a loose head scarf that drapes down her shoulders and to the middle of her back. She's straining to pull the bucket up and looks like she might just fall into the well.

When our eyes meet, I feel the air go out of my chest. In a flash, I realize all the terrible things I've been hearing are true. If she's here, it means she's married to the warlord now. As impossible as it sounds, she's his wife.

Rahima drops the rope, and the bucket whizzes back into the well, clanking and thudding against the brick walls as it drops into the dark earth.

Twenty-Three

"What are you doing here?" she whispers.

I stare at her. I can't help it.

She is thinner. Her eyes keep darting behind her and down the road. She seems terrified. Her dress hangs on her body awkwardly, and her shoulders are hunched forward.

"I needed to see you."

"You shouldn't be here."

Her hair is the only thing about her that doesn't look like a girl, and that's covered with the head scarf. Her eyes, her lips, her neck—all her features are so delicate. She looks nothing like Rahim.

"I went to your home."

Rahima steps out of the compound, pulling the door

closed behind her so no one will see us.

"You didn't come back to school, and I was really worried. When your sister told me I couldn't believe it."

"Everything happened so fast," she says. She blinks back tears, her lashes fluttering.

"That boy who answered the door—is he going to tell someone I'm here?"

Rahima shakes her head.

"He's more interested in playing before his father gets back."

"Is his father . . . Is he the one?"

Rahima looks away. I can see her face get red. I've never seen her this way. She looks like she might scream or sob. I touch her arm. She's trembling.

"But what about school? Your teachers will fail you if you don't come back! And Abdullah and Ashraf—they want to see you. I need you!"

My best friend looks like I just punched her in the stomach.

"Please come back."

"I can't," she whispers and takes a deep breath. "I hate this, Obayd. I hate my dress. I hate where I sleep. I miss my sisters and my mother. I don't want to be here."

I am angry for her. How could this have happened to someone like Rahim? Where is the *bacha posh* who taught me how to stand without falling? I want to save her.

"We can go now," I whisper, even though I'm not sure it's all that easy. "Come with me. You would never have to come back here!"

"You don't understand. They'll find me."

"Why are you acting like this? You would never let me give up. You would tell me to run!"

"Obayd!" She's angry now, a sad kind of angry. She sounds more like my best friend. "There are guards here. And where would I go? If I go home, they'll bring me right back and it'll only be worse. I can't run into the mountains. They'll find me."

"Why did this happen?"

"Why? Because I'm a girl. Because people think they can do what they want to us. They think we should have no say in what happens to us. That's why I don't want to be a girl. That's why I would've done anything to make myself a boy forever."

I think back to our trek to the mountains. How she wanted to keep going even after that snake had slid around my ankle, even though it was dark and we were nervous we wouldn't find our way home. My friend had bigger demons chasing her. I get that now.

"You knew this was going to happen."

She says nothing.

"Why didn't you tell me?"

"How could I tell you . . . *this*?" Her voice is small. She wipes a tear with the back of her hand and sniffles. She doesn't look as tall as I remember. I can't believe how much things have changed in just a few days.

I bite my bottom lip to keep it from shaking.

"What am I supposed to do without you?" It's a selfish thought, but I really feel lost without her.

"If I had one more day out there . . ." she says, looking at the world behind me, the world that's now out of her reach. "If I had one more day out there, I would spend every minute of it finding a way to make sure I never ended up in here."

It's my best friend talking to me in that way that's just for us. The look in her eye, the hidden words, the way she points somewhere over my shoulder with the tilt of her head. It's a code that no one else would understand, not even Abdullah or her sister Shahla. There are some things about Rahima that only I can understand.

"That's what I would do, Obayd," she says, fishing into the folds of her dress. She pulls out her Wizards hat and holds it out to me. It is folded in half, and the rim is bent in the wrong direction. "You should take this."

"Your Wizards hat?"

She nods.

"Why would you give that to me? You need it more than I do!"

"You've been staring at this hat since the first day I met

you." She smiles. "Maybe it's time for it to bring you some luck. And you know me. I'm not going to stay here forever. I'll tell you something, Obayd. These people aren't very bright. I'll find a way to outsmart them, even if it's not today."

I take the hat, even though I'm not sure I should. It feels strange to take something so important from her, especially at a time like this.

I'm touching the red embroidery and thinking about giving it back to her when I hear a hum in the distance.

We both turn and see a cloud of dust down the road. Somewhere in that cloud are black jeeps and somewhere in those black jeeps is a man that calls Rahima his wife.

"Obayd, you need to leave now!" She pulls her head scarf over her face and reaches for the door handle. "Go, Obayd! Please!"

She looks so afraid that I start to shake. She's inside again. She's closing the door, and all I can see is one wide eye.

The jeeps are getting closer. I can see a smudge of black in the center of the dust clouds.

"But what should I do without you, Rahim? What should I do?"

"Do everything," she says and closes the heavy door. Her voice calls out again—louder. "Do everything, Obayd! DO EVERYTHING!"

Twenty-Four

There are three jeeps and they are coming at me. I look around. Other than Abdul Khaliq's compound, there's nothing around here. There are no other homes, no shops or trees to hide behind. There is only the road.

I step away from the door. My friend is gone. She has probably ducked back into the house so her husband won't guess she came out. I don't know what it's like living in that house, but I could almost guess by the look on her face.

There's nothing beyond the compound. The road sort of ends here. If his guards see a boy walking into the open plain, they'll be curious enough that they'll come after me. I take a deep breath and decide there's only one way to go.

I put the Wizards hat on my head and tug the bent rim so it'll hide my eyes.

I walk back down the road, toward the jeeps, with their big tires and dark windows. I'm dressed in my pantaloons and tunic shirt. I have a men's vest on, one my father used to wear. It's big on me but makes me feel like a small man. The jeeps are close enough that they can see me, even if I can't see them. I walk, keeping my eyes straight ahead like I've got nothing to be scared of.

The first jeep whizzes past me and doesn't stop. It drives all the way around to the side of the compound and disappears from view. The second jeep slows as it comes close to me. If I reached my arm out, I would touch it. I can feel dust in my nose and throat. The jeep is inching along, slowly enough that I can't help turning and looking at the black window. I wonder if he's looking back at me, my best friend's husband.

The second jeep keeps going and I think I might be safe. Maybe they've decided a little boy is nothing to worry about. Maybe they think I've lost my way and wandered out this far by mistake. But if they ask me any questions, they'll know I'm lying.

The second jeep pauses a few yards from the compound.

I can hear its engine behind me.

I'm not surprised that the third jeep pulls up next to me. I keep walking, but when it stops abruptly I feel my stomach drop. I stop walking not because I want to talk to anyone but because I think it might be worse if I don't.

I don't know what to do with my eyes. It feels like forever before the black window slides down.

"What are you doing here?"

I look up at the bearded man talking to me. He's wearing a small wool cap, and I can see the long black neck of a rifle between his knees.

"Sorry."

"I bet you are. But I asked what you're doing out here."

There are two other men in the backseat of the jeep. They lean toward the window to get a better look at me. I can't see their faces well, and I'm not really trying. I try to keep my eyes on my sandals.

"Are you going to answer?"

There's one thing I've heard about the warlord, which is that he wears only black. The men in the jeep are dressed in beige, so I guess they must be his guards. Abdul Khaliq is probably in the second jeep, the one that's waiting right up by the compound, to see what the people in the third jeep learn about the mysterious boy wandering around his home.

"I'm on my way home now," I say. My voice is broken and dry from the dust and nerves.

The man looks at the other two guards in the car and shakes his head. He opens the door and steps out.

I half expect my best friend to come running out of the compound, shouting for these men to let me go and saving me from whatever's about to happen. But she doesn't. She can't.

"Little boy, what are you doing out here? It's a simple question."

He's much taller than me. My hands are sweaty and trembling. I'm ready to scream and run, though I won't get far. I consider crying and begging for mercy. How could a ten-year-old girl dressed as a boy possibly stand up to a warlord's guards? I've been a *bacha posh* for less than six months. That's not long enough to be as brave as Rahim!

I should fall apart, but I don't.

"I was sent here with a task," I say. "And I must apologize because I've done something pretty dishonorable."

"What task?" His nose wrinkles up, like he's trying to sniff out the truth.

"My family is very thankful to the great Abdul Khaliq for his help in keeping us safe. We are so appreciative. My mother baked a rosewater cake this morning, and my father asked me to bring it here. I've been walking for hours; at least, I think it's been hours. I didn't know how far this was from the market."

"So where is it?" He frowns at me.

"Where is what?"

"The cake. Where's the cake?"

"Oh, I was getting to that. You know, she was up before dawn mashing that dough with her fists. We could smell it baking and begged her to give us just a small piece, but she refused even my father. He loves her cakes, so he was really mad when she said no, no, no—"

"What are you talking about?"

"The cake. That's why I was apologizing. My mother was in such a hurry to send me out the door this morning that she forgot to give me any breakfast. When I got here, I knocked on the door a few times, but no one answered. I didn't want to be a bother, so I sat down and thought I might wait for someone to show up."

One of the men inside the jeep groans in frustration.

"Do we have to listen to this babbling?"

"Little boy, who's your father?"

"My father?" I don't want to answer that question.

"Yes, your father! I want to know who to blame for your existence!"

"My father's the angriest man in town. That's who he is. Follow me home and you'll see for yourself. Oh, I really don't want to tell my father what happened to the cake!"

"What are you talking about? Give me a straight answer before I knock it out of you!" he roars with a hand raised threateningly.

"I ate it!" I blurt out.

"You what?"

"I ate the cake."

He sighs, rubbing his forehead with his palm.

"It was a shameful thing to do and I'm so very sorry, but I couldn't help myself. I thought I might pass out after such a trek to get here and especially since I hadn't eaten anything before I set out, which was a big mistake, of course . . ."

The man turns to the two guards still in the jeep. "Is this real?"

One rolls his eyes and the other falls back against the seat and out of view.

"And now I think I'm going to be sick. My stomach's been pretty queasy since yesterday." I cross my hands over my belly and shift my weight on my feet. "You know that feeling when something doesn't want to be in there any-more but you're not sure which way it's going to come out?"

"The kid's an idiot. Let's move."

I don't stop. I keep going.

"I don't know what I'm going to tell my parents. They're going to kill me when they find out what I've done. That cake might have been the last thing I'll ever eat. Oh, you don't know my mother. This is the end of me!"

I am shaking my head as if home is what I dread instead of these black jeeps. I put my hands on my thighs and lean over as if I might throw up right at their feet.

"The last time I did something like this, my mother sent me to my uncle's house. She said she didn't know what she would do to me if I were around her. She's going to be out of her mind this time. I think I should probably just walk back to the market and pick up a cake from the bakery and bring it here. At least I could tell her I'd delivered a cake here, and that much of it would be the truth. It won't be the same, though. My mother's cakes are so much better than the ones from the bakery. They aren't nearly as dry or—"

"Tell the kid to shut up! He's making me crazy."

"He's making me hungry."

"This makes you hungry? Are you insane?"

"Maybe the yeast was bad," I moan, holding my belly. "Do they put yeast in cakes? I think I might be allergic to yeast."

There's the sound of static and a *click*. One of the men in the jeep has a walkie-talkie. A voice crackles through. I can't hear what the voice is saying, but I hear one of the men respond.

"We're coming in now. Just some idiot kid. He says he ate a cake he was supposed to deliver. If we don't leave him now, one of these guys is going to shoot him."

I should wet my pants right now, but by some miracle I don't.

The crackly voice on the walkie-talkie returns. This

time I stop talking so I can hear it.

"A cake? Tell the big-eared kid to keep his cakes. Who has time for this nonsense?"

The man waves at me and climbs back into the jeep. I nod and look as apologetic as I can. I walk away, kicking at the ground like I'm not eager to get home. The jeep takes off and when I turn around to look behind me, they've all disappeared behind the clay walls of the compound.

I take off running. I want to get as far away as possible.

And as I run I can't help thinking just how wild it is that I was able to talk my way out of being caught by the warlord's guards. Me, a little girl dressed in boys' clothes . . . How did I do that? It was like I wasn't myself, like I was someone else!

It was . . . it was . . .

And then it hits me. My hand touches Rahim's hat, fitting so snugly on my head that it doesn't fly off even as I race down the dirt road.

It was magic.

Twenty-Five

I won't take it off.

I knew there was something special about this hat. It made Rahim the way he was, tall and strong. What I didn't know was that the Wizards hat could share some of that with me, too.

I laugh, even though I'm alone. I can't help it. Every time I think about what I'd said to those guards, the frustrated looks on their faces, thinking I might actually vomit on their jeep—or worse.

My friend is right. Those people are not very smart.

"What are you laughing about?"

I spin around, my face red. Meena is behind me with her hands on her hips. She looks intrigued.

"Nothing."

She doesn't believe me. So I adjust the hat on my head and pick up my yellow schoolbag with the green truck painted on the front pocket. I pull the strap over my shoulder.

"Are you hiding something?" she asks with narrowed eyes. Meena doesn't give up. That's her thing.

"Why do you think I'm hiding something?" I ask as if her question is ridiculous—which it kind of is. I'm a girl dressed as a boy. I'm always hiding something.

I walk past her and know she's following me with her eyes. She won't let this go, and I don't want her finding out I made a trip to the warlord's compound four days ago. And if she finds out, I don't think she'll be able to keep it to herself. My parents will never let me out of the house if they learn what I've done. I have to stay cool.

"It's late, Meena. We should go."

Our walk to school is quiet except for Alia's moaning about a dress she saw one of the girls at school wearing.

"It's sooo pretty! I've never, ever, ever seen a dress like that before! You should've seen the colors. It was a different kind of blue—not like a bird's egg or Mother's ugly handbag. It was like a *queen's* blue. I wish, wish, wish I could have a dress like that!" Alia's being extra dramatic today. It should help take the attention off me.

Meena is listening to Alia, but she keeps an eye on me.

She's still not letting it go.

The warlord's guards could learn a thing or two from my sister.

"See you guys after school," I say with a wave when we get to the school grounds. I'm relieved to be in my classroom, sitting next to boys who don't see through me the way my sister does.

"You're wearing the hat!"

Abdullah spots it immediately. School has just let out, and Abdullah and Ashraf are standing in front of me. There's a big hole in our friendship since Rahim's gone. We were only really friends because of Rahim. Without him, we don't have much to talk about. I go back to feeling like a little kid around the big boys.

"Yeah."

"How'd you get his hat?" Ashraf asks.

People sure do have a lot of questions for me today.

"He gave it to me."

"When?" Abdullah steps closer to me.

"Last Friday."

"How?"

I'm kind of enjoying how baffled they are. Yes, Rahim was their friend before he was mine. Yes, they are boys, real boys. Yes, they are three or four years older than me, taller than me, bigger than me. And yes, it's me who actually had the guts to go find our best friend and try to do something about her being taken away.

"I went to him."

"You don't mean . . ."

"Yes, I went to his home."

Abdullah's eyes go wide. Ashraf sits on a big rock.

"You're not serious."

"I am. I wanted to talk to him."

"So, is it true?" Ashraf looks up at me and asks.

"Is what true?"

He and Abdullah look at each other. They're asking me something I don't want to talk about. I don't want to talk about Rahim as a girl, much less as a bride. And while I know they ignored the fact that Rahim was a *bacha posh*, I'm not sure if they know about me. They've never said a word about it either way.

"About Rahim. That he's not really a—that his father married him to the warlord?"

My friend would scream and kick if she could hear us talking about her like this.

"It's none of my business." That's the best answer I can come up with at this moment, but it's not good enough.

Abdullah shakes his head.

"We're his friends. I think it's very much your business and our business too," he says gently.

"We're not going to say anything," Ashraf adds. "If

that's what you're worried about."

So they know.

I nod. I can't summon the courage to admit anything about myself out loud. It's hard to go from keeping something a secret to talking openly about it outside of school.

"Where did you go?"

"I went to the compound. It's all true and it's awful. Her father married her off to the warlord."

"How is she?" Abdullah is really concerned. And I know he probably wishes he'd gone looking for her instead of me. I realize things are different now. I'm not just a little kid who Rahima brought around. The boys are talking to me like I'm one of them.

"She's okay but not really. I don't know. I didn't get to talk to her long. The guards there stopped me. I thought they were going to kill me."

"Guards? No way!"

I tell them all about the guards and how I threatened to get sick right there in front of them. I told them about their guns and dark jeeps.

"Why didn't she run away?"

"I don't know. I told her to, but she said they would have caught her."

"I think I'd run if I were her," Ashraf boasts.

"That's easy to say from here," Abdullah fires back then

turns to me. "What about you, Obayd? What are you going to do now?"

And then there's another person standing with us. Someone who just stepped out from behind the mulberry tree of the schoolyard. Someone who's heard every word of our conversation and gives me a look so accusing and harsh that it just about knocks me over.

"Yeah, Obayd. What are you going to do now?" Meena says.

Twenty-Six

"Meena, don't say anything to Mother . . . please!"

"I can't believe you went to the warlord's home! Are you crazy? And then you tease his guards like that? You're seriously out of your mind and Madar-*jan* is going to lock you up for sure."

"Meena, please!"

We are walking home. Alia is saying nothing. This is too much drama even for her taste.

"Obayd, that's really dangerous. You can't do stuff like that!"

"I know, Meena. I'm not going to go back there. I promise! Just don't say anything to Madar-*jan*. There's no point getting me in trouble, is there? It's all over, I swear."

"That's where you got that hat? I remember seeing your friend wearing it," she points out.

I put both hands on the rim protectively.

"Drop it, Meena."

"That's so dangerous!" Alia says, her chin trembling. She looks like she's going to start crying now.

Meena shakes her head.

"I can't believe it. They really did that to your friend? The warlord? She's so young!"

"I know. It's just awful."

Meena stops suddenly and faces me. Alia sniffles and wipes a couple of tears with the back of her hand. We wait for Meena to speak.

"Do you think the same thing is going to happen to you, Obayd? Because it's not. Our parents would never do something like that."

"How do you know? Have you ever asked them?"

I guess that's one of the things I've been secretly worried about. If Rahima's parents could arrange her marriage, maybe my parents would do the same thing.

"Is that what you're thinking? Are you nuts? Obayd, they would never do that to you or to any of us. Neela's sixteen years old, and they told her they wouldn't even think about letting her get married for a while. We're all younger than Neela, especially you."

She looks really sure of herself and makes a pretty

convincing argument, but maybe that's because she hasn't seen what I've seen. Still, I'd like to believe what she believes. I'd like to think my mother and father would not throw me into some man's house and expect me to survive—because I don't know if I could. I've been thinking about Rahima a lot. Maybe too much.

"Obayd," Meena says, her voice softer than it was just a minute ago. "Maybe you should talk to Madar about these things. Have you told her what's happened to your friend?"

"No."

"Why not?"

I fold my arms across my chest. I don't need my sister telling me what to do. She couldn't possibly understand the situation the way I do. She's only a girl.

Meena huffs with her hands on her hips.

"Obayd. Why not?" she repeats, exasperated. It's not my fault she's annoyed. It's her own fault that she can't let things go.

"We're going to be late," I say as I start walking down the road. Alia trails behind me.

I stop when I notice that Meena is right behind me. I steal a glance at her and realize she's got a tight-lipped, serious look on her face. My heart sinks when I realize what she's going to do. I whip around and grab her by the shoulders.

"Meena, you can't." I try to sound like I'm giving her an order, but it comes out more like a plea.

"I can't what?" my sister answers, slowly and deliberately. She's squinting at me, daring me to go on.

"Please don't tell Madar-*jan* about this. She can't know about this. They'll be too worried. Or they'll just kill me for going out there. Please, Meena."

Alia bites her lip.

"Maybe Obayd's right, Meena," she says quietly. "You know what'll happen to her if you tell. Do you really want to do that?"

Meena's face goes slack, like a balloon pricked by a needle. She stomps her foot.

"Fine, Obayd. But you have to promise that you won't go back there. And that you won't do anything that crazy, or I'll tell Madar-*jan* everything and I won't feel sorry one bit, whatever happens."

If Meena were a boy, we'd shake hands on it. Instead, I just nod. My sister links her arm with mine. Alia comes up on Meena's other side, and they lock elbows too. And that's how we go home. Almost like I'm their sister.

Twenty-Seven

Ever since I left Abdul Khaliq's compound, I've known exactly what I need to do. I'm going to do what Rahima would do if she were still Rahim.

If I had one more day out there, I would spend every minute of it finding a way to make sure I never ended up in here.

It's been more than two weeks since I went to the compound, and each day that's passed has felt like wasted time. I've got to find the waterfall. I've got the Wizards hat, and as much as I hate to think of Rahima without it, I'm really thankful that she gave it to me. That's the kind of stuff a real best friend does.

My mother lays out squares of warm bread topped with smears of butter and coarse sugar sprinkled on top.

"Eat this," she says. "I bought fresh butter yesterday. Your father's starting to get some pension payments because of his injury on the job. We're going to have a bit of income. It's not much, but at least we're not completely dependent on the family."

My mother worries. She worries about whether we're warm enough in the winter, about our grades in school, about what to feed us and what to do about my father's family. She worries a lot more than I ever realized. I didn't think she had a thing, but she definitely does, and worrying is it.

That's why this piece of good news seems to have her in a much better mood this morning. She won't stop worrying about money, but at least she can worry a little less.

I eat the bread with a cup of tea with milk. If my mother knew what I was getting ready to do today, she would snatch the bread and fresh butter from my mouth and trap me in my room. But she doesn't know, so she makes me a second square when she sees how quickly I eat the first. I feel bad hiding things from her, but it's for her own good.

"I'm going to go to hang out with the boys, Madar-*jan*," I say as casually as I can. "There's a big soccer tournament today."

"Oh, really?" she says, rubbing her growing belly. "That sounds like a lot of fun."

I can't believe I didn't notice that thing for so long. It looks impossible to hide. I stare at the shape and wonder if it's a boy or a girl. I hope, for the kid's sake, that it's a boy, even though I'm guessing my parents will be so happy with a son that they'll probably forget my boy name.

I really need to get going.

"Yup." I wipe my mouth with the back of my hand and get to my feet before she can ask me any more questions. Or before I can tell any more lies. I plant a kiss on the top of her head, which makes her smile. "See you later."

Meena's in the courtyard outside. She looks up at me as I'm leaving. My heart starts to beat faster.

"See you in a little while, Meena." She opens her mouth as if she's about to ask me something and then clamps it shut abruptly. I guess she's figuring if she doesn't ask, she won't be responsible for anything dumb I might do.

I'm going to go to the waterfall. I've filled a crinkly plastic bottle with water, remembering how thirsty I was the last time I made the trek to the mountains. I want to leave early so I can get there while there's still enough light to see anything that might be slithering around underfoot.

I walk past the homes on our road and listen to small voices carrying over their privacy walls. I pass boys in the empty lot at the edge of our neighborhood playing soccer. I'm tempted to join them but remind myself that I've got a mission. I pass by the old man selling potatoes, leeks, and red onions out of a cart. I reach the edge of town and see the dry emptiness that lies between our town and the mountains that separate us from the rest of the world.

I start walking.

Yesterday, I spent some time with my father. Somewhere in the nonsense I talked about, I squeezed in a few questions that I should have asked him long ago. I learned three things:

Looking from the edge of town, the mountain range has a funny pattern. There are three mountains that, together, look like a two-humped camel sitting on the ground.

The mountain with the waterfall is the camel's head. And the waterfall is just around the bend by the camel's right ear.

The grasses and trees are signs of water.

When I see them, it's the most obvious thing in the world. It's almost like I can hear my father's voice. There are two big mountains. Humps. Then there's a valley where things go from khaki and dry to spotted with green. To the right of the valley, there's a smaller mountain with a flattish top. There's one peak on there that has to be the camel's ear. My eye follows the outline of the mountain and I can almost imagine nostrils and an eye on the downslope, like I'm looking at the profile of a camel's face. There are trees and yellow-green grasses on the peak, which look almost like wispy hairs.

That's it.

I laugh. I wish Rahim were here to see this.

I start to jog, knowing the day will pass more quickly than it should and there's a lot of ground to cover.

I reach the camel's head by noon, guessing by how high the sun is over my head. I'm trying not to think about how sweaty and tired I am. It's better to think about how much closer I am to the waterfall. I can see the trail Rahim and I had followed weeks ago and feel sorry for us, knowing how far off we were. We didn't have a chance.

I take another sip of water and remind myself that I can't finish it all before I get to the waterfall. It's the beginning of summer but already warm enough to make me sweat after being outside for just a few minutes. Just as I tilt my head back to drink, I feel a tickle on my foot.

I scream and jump. It's not the snake I expected to see.

I take a couple of steps backward, keeping my eyes fixed on the golden brown monster a few feet away. He doesn't move—like he's not sure what to do either. It's a standoff between me and the deadly scorpion that could have stung me.

"Don't you dare come near me," I mutter. There's no one around, but it feels better to be saying something out loud. I realize it'll feel even better to shout. "I'm warning you. I'll kill you!"

He looks like he's considering my threat and makes one of his own. His beaded tail is curled up behind him, poised and ready to turn me into a crying mess. I've never been bitten by a scorpion, but we're raised to fear them. I've heard that one sting from its tail can make a wrestler bawl for his mommy. He's standing between me and the camel's head.

I pick up a rock and throw it at him. He takes one tiny step back. I could walk around him, but I want him to be afraid of me. I want him to know he can't just crawl over my feet. I want to be in charge here.

"Get out of my way!" I scream and pelt three more rocks in his direction. The first is way off. The second is closer, and the third slams against his tail. He scampers off faster than I realized a scorpion could move, and I feel the tightness around my chest start to relax.

I had a scorpion on my foot and didn't get stung. My leg is not swelling into a purple balloon. I'm standing.

I take the Wizards hat off, wipe the sweat from my forehead, and slip the hat back on.

Thank you, Rahim. I think you just saved my life.

I keep moving.

Another hour passes before I reach the camel's head. I find a path that leads up to the camel's nostril and then forks off to the left, curling around the rock animal's ear. I make my way up the trail, the small rocks turning into bigger stones and boulders as I climb. I keep my eyes on the ground in front of me, watching for scorpions and snakes and anything else I should be afraid of. Every once in a while, I look up to see how far I've come.

That's when I hear it—a quiet hum. I've got snakes on my mind and freeze, scanning the ground for a sinister tail or beady eyes. I don't see anything, but the hum is still there. I keep walking, my heart pounding. The sound is making me nervous.

The hum gets louder. The trail gets steeper. The sun gets hotter.

I won't turn around. I'm going to make it. I imagine my next conversation with Rahima, even though I know there won't be one.

I did it, Rahima. I climbed all the way up to the camel's head and hiked around his ear. No, I wasn't afraid. Not one bit.

Then I know. The hum starts to sound wet and free. I climb over a patch of rocks and peer onto the other side to see the most amazing thing I've ever seen in my life.

Clear, cold water pours from the other side of the peak. It cascades down the rocky drop-off and lands in a pool below. It is beautiful and dangerous, a thrilling combination. I am tired and thirsty and open my mouth to catch the misty air on my tongue.

When I open my eyes, I see them.

Rainbows. There are a few of them, floating over the cascade of water. They hover in the air.

I climb down to where there's a ledge. From there, I'll be able to touch a rainbow. I move carefully, one foot at a time. I test each rock to make sure I won't lose my footing. It's a steep drop-off. I'd have better luck surviving a scorpion bite.

One rock rolls under my left sole and I gasp. I dig my hands into the wall. I walk sideways and relax as the ledge gets wider. I reach my right hand out and touch the stream of water. It tickles my fingertips, cold even on this warm day. I let it fill my palm, bubbly and cool, and bring it to my lips.

The rainbow is a step away.

I take a deep breath and put my right foot out, then my left. I am under the stream. The rainbow is over my head. My whole body is drenched in cold water. With one more step, I'm on the other side of the rainbow and the water. I see it hit the surface of the pool below in a foamy puff.

You should have seen it, Rahima. The water and rainbows, the way the water fell off the mountain—it was the coolest place. The rocks were huge, and the drop was so steep. I've never seen a place so perfect and frightening at the same time.

I yell. My boy voice echoes against the rocky walls and slips into the opening that is the camel's ear. It is not the voice of a girl dressed as a boy. It is even stronger. Invincible. My hands are clenched into fists, and when the cool mist of the waterfall touches my face, it sends an electric wave pulsing through my body.

In this secret, hidden place, something magical has happened.

Twenty-Eight

"Where have you been? Why are you wet? You're going to get sick walking around like that! Have you lost your mind?"

My mother is mad. Not the kind of mad that goes away quickly. She's the kind of mad that boils over onto my sisters, too, which means the whole house is going to be mad at me. She's the kind of mad that can't even decide how to punish me. She's the kind of mad that I never want to see, and I expected her to be like this. So why did I do it?

Because I had to.

I knew she would be mad because it took me forever to get back. My clothes were sopping when I left the waterfall. I climbed back onto the mountain path to a small clearing and fell asleep with my head on a rock. When I woke up, the sun had sank low in the sky, and I was still a long way from home.

"I'm very sorry, Madar-*jan*." I hang my head low, but my voice stays steady. Usually when I'm in trouble, I get so nervous that I start to cry. I don't mean that I bawl my eyes out, but I do get teary-eyed. Not this time.

"Sorry? What is that supposed to mean? I asked you where you've been and you just say sorry?"

My sisters have come out of the bedroom. I see them in the shadowy hallway, timid in their pajamas. They are probably glad I'm here so they don't have to be yelled at for my behavior. I hope her shouting doesn't wake my father. I really don't want him upset with me. When he gets mad, I always feel really bad, like I did something to hurt him worse than he's already been hurt.

"I was outside playing, and I fell asleep."

"You fell asleep. That's it?"

Her eyes are wide. She's got one hand on her hip and one on her forehead. Her mouth is half-open. Maybe she's not that mad, after all? Maybe she's just surprised.

"Yes, Madar-*jan*. We ran a lot playing soccer, and it must have tired me out more than I thought. I was just going to sit down for a few minutes. I don't know what happened. When I woke up, I was really surprised it was so dark."

"You fell asleep," she repeats. Her voice is lower. I haven't heard my father stirring yet. His hearing seems to be a lot worse than I thought it was. That man could sleep through a thunderstorm. At this particular moment, I'm grateful for that.

"Yes. I promise I'll never do it again. I'll change and go to bed now."

"Have you lost your mind?" she says at full volume. My stomach drops. My father is going to holler from his bed. Any second now.

"Look at these clothes!" My mother's got her hands on my shirt. My jeans are dark and damp. If the sun had been out, they might have had a chance to dry before I came home.

"Mother!" I snap, pulling away from her. My voice is deeper than I remember it. I guess that's part of the changing process. I'm guessing it's something that happens slowly, since I still feel like I've got a girl's body. "I said I was sorry. I'll go change. Let everyone get to sleep."

"What's gotten into you? You've been missing for hours. I've been going crazy worrying, thinking you might be dead, and you show up wet and acting like . . . like . . . like some spoiled prince?"

I'm definitely not spoiled, I want to tell her.

"You're going to tell me right now where you've been or you're going to spend the next few years without seeing daylight." She means every word of it. The lamp flickers nervously—it doesn't doubt her threat.

I take a deep breath. Why not tell her? I might as well let her know that I've finished what she started. Six months ago, she made me into a *bacha posh*, but in that time I've made myself into a boy. She won't have to worry about not having a son anymore. I can start doing the things my two-legged father used to do for us, like earning money or nailing a leg back onto a chair. All the things people say about our family not having a boy won't be true anymore. The more I think about it, the more I want to tell her. She'll be so grateful!

"I went to the waterfall up on the mountain."

My mother crumples to the cushion on the floor. Her hands are on her belly.

"The mountain? For God's sake, Obayd, what were you doing on the mountain?"

"Have you ever tried finding a rainbow? No, not just finding it but actually reaching it? It's so strange. They're always a little farther away. You go and go and then somehow it's to your left instead of in front of you or it's gone but you can never look up and pass right under it."

My sisters are in the everything room now. This is too good to miss.

"But I found the waterfall. I found it on my own! I mean, Padar told me where it was, but I went there by myself."

Alia's got a strange look on her face like I'm speaking a language she doesn't understand. Then I look over and see, by the moonlight, that Neela and Meena have the same look on their faces. I feel the divide between my sisters and me widening. They're girls. They couldn't possibly imagine how I did this. I can't help but smile just a little. That look on their faces, that distance between them and me, is proof my plan is working.

"I passed under a rainbow, Madar-*jan*. Can't you tell? Can't you see there's something different about me? The rocks were slippery and the water was cold, but the rainbow was there—close enough to touch."

"Obayd, I've told you how important it is to always tell me the truth."

"That is the truth!"

My mother is hunched forward, her fingers pressing on her temples. She's upset, but not the way she was a few minutes ago.

"Please tell me a better truth than that."

"A better truth? This is what you wanted, isn't it? Didn't you want me to be a boy? Mother, that's the only way we knew to make it real. We had to pass under the rainbow so the change would be forever."

I said *we*. As if Rahima hadn't disappeared from my life. As if she'd been there with me, toeing over rocks and feeling the spray of cold, mountain water.

"Obayd, Obayd, Obayd," she moans. "That's a legend. It's a story we tell children, but it's not true. Why would you believe such a thing? Nothing happens when you pass under a rainbow."

I am furious with her and wonder if she remembers that she's the one who thinks always telling the truth is so important. She *should* remember. She said that only a few seconds ago.

My sisters are sullen but for different reasons. Neela is picking at imaginary lint on her skirt. She feels responsible for everything we do because, as the oldest, she's been told so often that she is. I can tell Meena feels guilty for hiding from Mother that I'd gone to the warlord's compound and is waiting for that bombshell to explode. Alia is on the brink of tears because she can't stand to see me in trouble or to see Mother so enraged.

I don't want them to look the way they do. The sooner I prove my point, the sooner we can get back to normal.

"How do you know, Mother? Have you ever passed under a rainbow? Why would everyone keep telling the legend if it weren't at least a little true? And besides, I know it worked. I can already feel it."

My mother looks at me like I've grown a second head.

"Obayd, the only thing that's different about you is that you're soaked and probably going to wake up with pneumonia. We thought something terrible had happened to you. Do you have any idea how worried we were?" She leans back and shakes her head. "What have I done? I didn't think you would ever . . . I thought you knew this dressing as a boy was just for a while. It was never meant to be forever. Why would you want to be a boy forever?"

"Why would you want me to be a boy only for now? If being a boy now is good, isn't being a boy forever even better?"

She says nothing, but her lips pull together and nearly disappear, so I know I've said something touchy. I just can't tell if it's good or bad.

"Mother, can we just go to bed? I promise not to go anywhere without telling you again."

"Just go to bed? As if nothing happened?" My mother's voice is loud and shrill. I look toward the hallway and wait for my father to yell at us for waking him. I'm pretty sure my mother hasn't told him I've been missing. She's been hiding things from him lately—things that might upset him.

"Mother, please," I whisper, hoping she'll take the hint and lower her voice. "I'm really, really sorry."

Just then the front door bursts open. I look up and my mouth falls open stupidly. I'm scared and shocked and confused all at once. How could this be? I blink and think, for a split second, that tonight is surely a night of magic and my mother must be a fool not to see it. There, with one foot on the ground and his stump on the wooden crutch I made for him, stands my breathless, sweating father.

Twenty-Nine

"Obayd!" My name comes out in an exhausted bellow. Right after he says it, my father wipes his forehead with the back of his hand.

I just stare at him, watching him balance his weight on his crutch. I'd almost forgotten how tall my father is.

"Father, you're using it! You're walking!" I'm on my feet and clapping. "It works, doesn't it? How far did you go?"

"Obayd!" my mother snaps. "Look how exhausted you've made your father, and you're going on and on as if . . ."

"Mother," I huff, thinking how hard it is to explain things to parents sometimes. "Are you seeing him? He's walking."

My father takes a few steps into the room. He gets himself to the floor cushions and Neela stands up. He drops the walking stick to the floor and supports himself with a hand on Neela's arm. He slides down the wall and sits with his leg and stump stretched out in front of him.

"Ask him where he went," my mother dares. "Go ahead and ask this child of yours where he was today."

"Obayd, I've been out looking for you for hours. Your mother was convinced you were dead! Do you have any idea what you've put us through?"

Hours? Hours? This is incredible! I hop from foot to foot in a small celebration. If only I could share this good news with Rahima. She would be so happy!

"You were out there for hours? Padar-*jan*, that's wonderful! Was the ledge okay? I wasn't sure if I'd put enough padding on it, but I guess if you—"

"Padding? How can you be talking about padding? Do you not hear what I'm saying?" My father's head thumps against the wall.

My mother pours my father a glass of water from a metal pitcher. She's shaking her head.

"Obayd, you've lost your mind."

"The height is just right. I can't believe it. You know, we did that without measuring. I just tried to picture you standing next to me and guessed . . ."

My parents look at each other. My sisters drop their

heads in one synchronized motion. I stop bouncing around from foot to foot. When I see their eyes sneaking glances from lowered eyelids, it occurs to me I might actually be in more trouble than I've realized.

I stiffen. The air in the room is tense. My stomach drops, as it probably should have a long time ago.

"Obayd, this has to end," my mother says grimly. "This has gone too far."

My breath catches. *What has to end?*

My father rubs at his thigh and grimaces.

"Right now. As of this moment, Obayda. There will be no discussion about it. No questions. No complaints."

Obayda? It takes me a moment to realize she's talking to me. She can't be serious. I barely recognize that name anymore.

"Mother . . ." I start, but she cuts me off with a sharp look.

She wants to stand up, which takes a good amount of effort. Her belly has gotten big in the last month. Rising is not a quick process, and involves lots of knees and elbows and huffing.

"I will take care of this right now. To have you walking in here talking about rainbows and crazy legends and . . . and . . . and padding! Of all things . . . padding!" My mother storms off down the hallway as fast as two people packaged in one can possibly move. While I should be wondering what my mother is going to do, I'm stuck thinking how much of this is happening because of that baby.

My sisters are staring down the short hallway. Three curious necks crane after her. My father's eyes are closed. Today has taken a year's worth of energy out of him. This is my doing, and I feel mostly bad about that. I have to admit, though, that part of me is thrilled that I got him out of the house.

I refuse to stand still. I follow my mother. She said I couldn't ask any questions or complain, but she didn't say I couldn't tag along to see what she was going to do.

She goes into the room I share with my sisters. She sidesteps the floor cushions and opens the cardboard box in the corner of the room. She pulls out a green plastic bag I thought we'd never open again.

"Mother, no!"

She whips her head around and glares at me.

"You've got to listen to me, Obayda." She reaches into the bag and pulls out one of my three dresses. We packed these away the day she'd made me into a *bacha posh*. She's dead serious. "I'm doing this for your own good. We love you, and it's our responsibility to do the right thing for you. You'll be wearing a dress tomorrow morning."

The dress is a gloomy dark blue with spots where the detergent's done more than it should and leached the pigment out. It's wrinkled and probably too short, but I don't dare say that to my mother right at this moment. She takes my Obayd clothes, the pants I play *ghursai* in, the shirts I wear in the boys' classroom. She rolls them into a lumpy ball and tucks them under her arm.

"I thought you could have more time this way, but it's clear you can't handle it. The rest of the family will see you in a dress tomorrow, and all of . . . *this* . . . will be behind us. You'll behave respectably and come home straight after school. You'll be with your sisters in the afternoon and nowhere else. God, I wish there were a way to make your hair grow out this instant!"

She flings the dress on my sleeping cushion and raises one meaningful eyebrow.

"There's nothing else to discuss, Obayd. No, not Obayd!" My mother catches herself, but it's too late. She gapes at me, the wind knocked out of her angry outburst. She tries to recover but can't even do that gracefully. I stare at her. I can feel my chin trembling. The little voice inside me argues back with my mother.

"Don't answer to that name."

I didn't.

"You're Obayda."

Are you telling me or yourself?

"I know you're mad, but I thought . . . I thought you were dead. You don't know what you did to me."

I could say the same.

"Forget this boy stuff. It's all over now. By tomorrow, you'll be a new person. Or back to your old self. Whichever it is." She turns to leave.

It's finally too much for me. I burst into embarrassing girl tears.

Thirty

My chest feels tight and hard in a weird way.

There's a sliver of light coming through where the clay of the roof doesn't quite meet the clay of the wall. It's a slit that a pencil couldn't fit through, but the light comes in thin and seems to spread out. I stare into that light and wonder if what I'm feeling is an effect of walking under the rainbow or if it's because my parents have decided to turn my world upside down for the second time.

I run my hands down my arms and legs. I've got the Wizards hat under my head and can feel the rim pressed up against the back of my head. I'm thankful my mother didn't see the hat under my blanket. It would have been as gone as my pants and shirts.

"Are you asleep?" It's Alia, her voice a whisper. She sleeps on my left. I roll onto my side so I'm facing her. The room is dark, but by the sliver of light I can make out the shape of her face.

"No," I whisper back.

It is quiet for a moment. We can hear my father's snores through the thin wall. It's not the reason why I can't sleep. That's the sound I've been sleeping through all my life.

"Are you okay?"

I don't know how to answer that question. I should be okay. I haven't been stung by a scorpion. I haven't fallen off a ledge of wet rocks. I haven't been disowned by my parents. But I also don't know what I am. I really want to be a boy, but my mother's told me that's not going to happen because rainbows don't actually have powers. I refused to believe her and figured I'd start feeling more changes soon.

I went to the outhouse before I came to bed. I had to pee crouched down, just like always.

"Did you hear me? Are you okay?"

"I guess so."

"They're so angry," Alia says. "I've never seen Madar so upset! I thought she was going to rip her hair out. Do you think she's going to be mad forever?"

"No," I mumbled. I sigh at Alia's ability to make

everything sound worse than it is. "She wasn't that mad. Besides, I'm the one who should be upset. Not her."

"You?"

"Yes, me. I'm the one they want to make into a girl."

"You never ever complained about being a girl when you were one. Not once."

"You don't understand. You don't know what it's like. It's so much better being a boy."

I don't mean to sound like I'm talking down to her, but I don't know how else to tell her how I feel.

"Sometimes, Obayd or Obayda or whoever you think you are, sometimes you are a real hardhead." That's not Alia. That's Neela. Our whispering must have woken her.

"I am not," I say defensively.

"Yes, you are," Meena whispers angrily. "You never stop to think that maybe what you do comes back to us—especially when you're not around."

All four of us are awake.

"You just don't get it. None of you do."

"Why do you have to say that?" I can't tell if that was Meena or Neela. "Do you really think you're that different from us? You know it was just a pair of pants. That's all it was. Your hair will grow back. Nothing else about you changed. You were Obayda all along. You've always been a girl and you always will be."

It's Neela. Even in a hushed voice, she sounds more

like a mom than a daughter. I feel my face flush, realizing that I haven't been thinking of my sisters' feelings. This whole thing has been all about me. I remember the way they looked earlier in the night, sitting on the sidelines and watching. They'd probably had to sit through hours of my parents worrying and yelling. I think about what Meena just said. My mother must have asked if they knew where I was. I could picture Meena wondering if I'd gone back to the warlord's compound and debating whether she should tell my parents about it.

"I'm sorry," I tell them. Things haven't been fair to them ever since I became Obayd. I've probably known that for a while but ignored it because I could. My apology doesn't sound like much, even to me, but I do mean it. "I really am sorry. I just don't know what to do."

"There's nothing to do," Neela explains. "You just go back to being you."

"But don't you think . . ." I'm really glad it's dark in the room as I ask this question. "I went all the way to the mountain and passed under a rainbow. It wasn't the biggest rainbow, but it was there and I did it. Don't you think that's going to do something?"

"Honestly?" Meena says. "Maybe it did work. You were Obayd when you went there. The legend says it changes boys to girls and girls to boys. So maybe it changed you from a boy to a girl."

I roll onto my back and my eyes go wide. I hadn't thought of that possibility. Did I bring this girl-ness upon myself?

"Meena, what are you talking about? People don't just change like that. Rainbows can't change your . . . your body parts." Neela is careful with her words. None of us really wants to get into the real differences between girls and boys.

"But do the body parts matter?" Meena asks. "Are you a boy because you have those body parts or are you a boy because you get to do boy things?"

"Of course it's the body parts." Neela groans.

"I don't know," Alia replies. "Obayda didn't have the body parts, but she was a boy because she did all those boy things. She even made that crutch that Padar was using today. That was pretty neat, by the way."

"She wasn't *really* a boy. She was just pretending." Neela sounds so frustrated with us. I think that's just part of being the oldest, though.

"Everyone said she was a boy," Alia retorts. "And everyone treated her like one. And, even more importantly, she ate like one. I don't think I've had a single drumstick since she became Obayd."

Meena and Neela have to stifle their laughter.

"Is that what you're worried about? A piece of chicken?"

"The drumstick is the *best* piece," Alia says in her most wistful voice.

The room is quiet again. My sisters are probably thinking about drumsticks, but I'm thinking about what they've said.

Was I really a boy or was I just acting like one? That makes a big difference. Meena's theory about the rainbow turning me back into a girl isn't totally crazy, even if it does make my head spin just a little bit to think about.

It is starting to sink in, though, that this girl-ness is for real. The tightness in my chest is gone. I don't feel weird anymore. All I feel is sad that things are never going to be the way they were when it was me and Rahim. I reach behind my head and pull the Wizards cap on. I miss my best friend a lot tonight.

Thirty-One

"Madar?" I say quietly from the hallway. It is barely morning and my sisters are still fast asleep in our room. I snuck out without waking them. They didn't get much sleep last night, thanks to me.

I wish I could stick my hand into the everything room and feel out my mother's mood. I don't know if she's as angry as she was last night or if the hours between then and now have turned her from red hot to summery yellow. It's wishful thinking to imagine her a cool blue.

"Mm?" She looks up at me. She's hunched over a plastic tray of uncooked rice. She sifts through the rice with her fingertips, looking for the teeniest rocks that get missed when they bag the rice grains. She always does this, ever since Neela chipped a tooth when she bit down on one years ago. It occurs to me that Madar spends hours doing things like this for us, trying to make things as perfect as she possibly can. If she's decided to change me back into a girl, it's not because she wants to hurt me.

"I'm sorry about yesterday, Madar-*jan*."

Her eyes glisten and she lets out a soft sigh. That's all I need. I run over to her and bury my face in the soft space between her shoulder and her chest. I feel her arms wrap around me.

"I'm sorry too."

I want to ask what she's sorry about it but I'm afraid to. My mother nudges the tray of rice away and pulls me in closer. It's not easy, but somehow I snuggle up to her even with her round belly.

The sky outside is dark orange and yellow. The sun is still tucked behind the mountains.

I feel something push against my side where I'm nuzzled against my mother. When I feel it a second time, I pull back.

"What's that?"

My mother smiles and puts a hand on her belly.

"Did you feel it? That's the baby moving."

Could she have said anything crazier? The baby is deep in her belly and somehow managed to push at me.

"Really? Does it always do that?"

She nods and tilts her head in a way that tells me she's not red-hot mad anymore. She's not even yellow.

"Is the baby coming out soon?"

My mother purses her lips and thinks for a moment.

"I think it'll be another six or seven weeks," she says. "And things will be a little different then. Babies don't sleep much at night, and they cry. They are really small and need a lot of attention. But it might be good for your father to have a new baby at home."

"Only if it's a boy."

My mother pulls back and looks at me.

"What did you say?"

"Only if it's a boy," I repeat. "If it's a girl, I don't think you or Father are going to be happy at all. That was the whole point, wasn't it? You wish we'd been born as boys, so you made me into a boy."

My mother grips my shoulders and looks directly into my eyes. I feel my face flush, thinking I must have said something wrong to make my mother look at me so strangely.

"It was wrong, Obayda. It was very wrong of us to do that to you. I want you to understand that I know that now. Whatever reasons we came up with, it was the wrong thing to do. I wish you could have seen how happy your father was when each of his daughters was born."

I can't keep my mother's stare. I look down. I guess this

is her way of apologizing. It doesn't change anything, but it does make me feel a little better. I woke up yesterday as a boy. Today, I woke up as a girl who kind of looks like a boy. I'm either a totally new person or haven't changed at all. I can't really tell.

"Are you hungry?"

Just as my mother asks the question, my stomach lets out an attention-seeking growl. With everyone so worked up last night, I totally forgot to eat. My mother reaches to the small metal tray on the other side of her and butters a square of still-warm flatbread. She pulls a pinch of brown, coarse grain sugar from a ceramic bowl and sprinkles it over the butter. I take it from her and feel the sugar crystals melt on my tongue. The butter is salty, but that only makes the sugar taste even sweeter.

"Thank you," I mumble between bites.

"Your sisters are still sleeping?" My mother goes back to sifting through the grains of rice. There's just enough light in the room for her to see, but it's still dark enough that she's squinting a little. It's leaving a crease in her forehead, right between her eyes.

"They'll probably be up soon."

"I doubt it. You were all up most of the night whispering. I was surprised to see you awake this early."

I stop chewing and look at her from the corner of my eye.

"What were you girls talking about?"

I start chewing again so I won't be able to answer immediately. Thank goodness for my excellent manners.

"You're going to keep it a secret?"

"It was nothing. Can't even remember what we were talking about." I shrug.

I see the corners of my mother's mouth turn up, just enough to tell me she sees through my forgetfulness.

"Yes, I'm sure it was nothing," she confirms.

I lean up against my mother again, feeling especially close to her because she seems to have forgiven me for everything that happened yesterday. I feel a thump against my flank again.

"Whoa—that was a serious kick!"

"It sure was."

"With kicks like that, it must be one strong baby. Definitely a boy."

My mother stops sifting and takes a deep breath.

"Each one of you girls kicked just like that before you were born. At least that strong, if not stronger. You should know better than anyone not to assume a girl couldn't do that."

I break out into a full smile, teeth and all. Maybe it is a baby sister in there, and maybe she kicked me for thinking so little of her.

I hear three slow taps and realize the snoring has

stopped. It's my father. He's standing (STANDING!) in the hallway and poking his head into the everything room. He rests his weight on the walking stick and tries to finger-comb his bed head. It doesn't work.

"Good morning, Father." I stand up and walk toward him slowly. I'm just as excited as I was last night, but I'm afraid to start talking about the crutch. I need to see what kind of mood he's in this morning. There are no color signs on him, either.

"Good morning, Obayda," he says groggily. He keeps one hand on the crutch and reaches his other arm out toward me. I let his arm pull me to him, and he kisses the top of my head. I want to say something but am certain that if I try to make any sound at all, I will end up in tears. I couldn't say exactly why, but my chest is a bubble ready to pop.

"You're up early," my mother comments.

"I think all that fuss yesterday is still working its way through me," my father says. I've got my ear pressed against his chest and can feel the vibration of his words.

"I'm really sorry I made you worry. And I'm sorry you had to go looking for me." My voice is a squeak.

"It was unacceptable—something you must never, ever do again." His voice is deep and warm. The anger from yesterday has melted into a stern warning. I can breathe a little easier.

"I know. I won't do it again."

"Did you really go up to the waterfall?"

I nod slowly.

He lets out a soft moan.

"The things that could have happened to you. That's why you were asking me about the waterfall? If I'd known what you were planning, I never would have . . . But how did you find the water?"

"You told me how to find it, Padar-*jan*. I went to the camel's head. Everything was just like you said it would be. I found the ear, went behind it, and followed the sound of water."

"It's such a long way from here. And it's not an easy place to get to. There's barely a path, and it's rocky. You're lucky you didn't get bitten by a snake or . . . You really went alone?"

"Yes."

There is a moment of silence as the three of us imagine what could have gone wrong. I don't have to imagine that hard. I just think back to the creatures I saw along the way. I can almost feel the tickle on my foot even as I stand with my father.

"Put a jacket on, Obayda. The sun hasn't yet warmed the sky, and it's a little brisk outside."

There's a green sweatshirt on the wooden chair in the corner of the room. I slip one arm in, then the other.

"Do you need me to bring something from outside, Padar-*jan*?"

"Yes, *bachem*." It's nice to hear my father call me his child. For a daughter who was in deep trouble yesterday, I'm feeling awfully loved today. "We need water from the well, and I think some morning air would do us both good. How about a walk with your father?"

If he'd asked me that question yesterday, I would have been out the door before he could finish his sentence. But that was yesterday, when I was a different person. I look down at myself and see a dress that looks like it's on the wrong body. I outgrew it while I was a boy, but I know telling my mother that won't get me back into my boy clothes.

"But, Padar, what if people are outside? I look so strange with this dress and short hair. What will people think?"

"What do you think is a stranger sight to see—a girl with short hair or a ghost walking with a crutch? I promise, the only eyes that will be on you will be the ones wanting to see what magical child managed to drag a one-legged spirit out for a walk."

Thirty-Two

Under a sky ribboned in purple and gold, my father and I walk. We circle once around our neighborhood block. I remember racing Rahim from one corner wall to another, me chasing the dust clouds his plastic sandals raised from the ground. We walk past my uncle's home down the street and, over the wall, I hear my cousins just starting to wake. In a cry that would shame a rooster, my cousin yells that his brother has been sleeping too long. It is morning, he shouts, and only girls sleep this late.

My father and I look at each other and share a conspiratorial smile. Outside of the house and standing upright, I can see just how thin he is. His face is gaunt beneath the scruff he's grown. The hairs on his chin are peppered with silver. I don't remember seeing that before. His clothes hang limply with nothing to cling to. I remember what he said about being a walking ghost. I hate to think how perfect his self-description was.

From the corner of my eye, I watch him walking with the crutch. I remember the day he took me to the doctor to get checked. I remember walking with him to the pharmacy. He'd had to slow his step so I wouldn't fall too far behind. Today, his steps are short and I have to slow down so I won't get ahead of him.

His body swivels a little with each stride. He doesn't look totally comfortable. He stops every few yards and readjusts his stump or his grip on the crutch. I wait for him to tell me it's not a very good crutch or that he's too tired and wants to go back home.

He says neither of these things. He only takes a deep breath and starts again.

We walk beyond the four pomegranate trees with sad, barren branches and stop at the well. I've got a three-gallon plastic container and a funnel. The well is a metal neck that sticks out of a concrete square. The square is half as tall as I am and makes for a solid base. The metal of the pump is bright and looks out of place in our village. The neck sprouts a long lever on one end and a short, fat spigot on the other.

I put the funnel into the mouth of the plastic container and place it directly under the spigot. My father is watching me, not saying a word. He wipes his forehead with a handkerchief and works on catching his breath. I cringe to think how hard it must have been for him to roam the streets last night looking for me.

"I'll pump," my father says. He takes a few hop-steps to the long handle that sticks out parallel to the ground.

There is a green plastic chair by the well. My father looks exhausted, and we still have to get back home.

"Padar, why don't you sit? I can pump the water. It's usually my job anyway."

"No," he says, shaking his head. He takes a quick look around to see if anyone from our neighborhood is around to see him. No one is. He clears his throat and takes a deep breath. "I can do this."

It's been months since I've seen my father doing anything more than hobble from one room to another. I can't believe it's my walking stick that's gotten him this far.

He puts his hand on the lever and balances himself. He starts to push the lever down, but as he pushes toward the ground, he leans over. I take a quick step toward him, afraid he's going to tip over.

"No!" he yells out when he sees me getting near. It's not an angry yell. It's more like a panicked one. "I don't need help, *bachem*."

"I can do it, Padar . . ."

"I know you can. I know *you* can."

I get it then. I understand that my father needs to prove he can do this without his daughter's assistance. I shut my mouth and go back to the spigot.

With a grunt, he pushes the lever down. It's an undertaking made by his entire body. He lets the crutch drop to the ground and puts both hands on the lever. The veins in his neck bulge with every push. I hear a gurgle in the pipe and see a wet sputter at the spigot's mouth.

"It's coming, Padar! It's coming!"

I'm cheering him on as if gold has spewed from the spigot instead of water. But it's not just water. It's much more than that, as proven by looking at the broad smile on my father's ruddy face.

When the container is full, we decide to rest. My father lets himself fall into the plastic chair. I sit on the concrete base of the pump. My feet dangle just a few inches off the ground.

"Obayda, do you remember the day in the market? The day I lost my leg?"

That day is not a day we ever talk about.

I feel my stomach churn at the mention of that day. How could I possibly forget it when it had all started with that bottle of medicine? I can't look at my father's leg without hearing the screaming, smelling a world on fire, and seeing my father torn to pieces. It's the blackest, ugliest day I've ever seen, and I don't think it'll ever get even a little fuzzy in my mind. But that's not how I answer my father.

"I remember."

The sky is more gold than purple now. I can hear a dog yelping in the distance. The world is waking.

"It was a terrible day. I wish more than anything that I could go back and change things—if only we'd left the house a half hour earlier or gone to the pharmacy on the other end of the market. But none of that can be changed and no one is to blame for that other than the people who exploded that car there."

My throat is thick and hot. I stare at my feet because I don't know what will happen if I look up. Something in me feels lighter, though. I hadn't realized, until this moment, just how bad I felt about being the reason for my father's injury. I concentrate on taking slow, steady breaths as he continues.

"I only remember the first part of that day. I remember looking at you sitting on a bench across the road. I remember my arm going up to wave at you and I remember you waving back. I remember the green-and-white dress you were wearing. I remember the way your bangs were tucked behind your ear. That's the last thing I remember, and I'm glad my mind stopped recording then, with my eyes on your face. After that, there's nothing but black until the next day, when I woke up and your mother was sitting next to me, crying."

I nod. My father is lucky not to remember anything that happened after the explosion. I wish I didn't remember either.

"All the days after that—the pain where my leg should have been and everywhere else, the fevers, the look on your mother's face when she saw me. I couldn't bring myself to talk. I wanted to be alone. I asked your mother not to bring any of you to the hospital."

"She told us the doctors didn't think it was a good idea for us to visit."

"The doctors didn't say a thing about it. It was my idea."

I look up at him curiously.

"Why did you do that?"

"I couldn't bear to look at you girls. I've been your father your whole life, but when I woke up and realized what had happened to me, I knew I couldn't be your father the way I wanted to be. I couldn't work or pay our rent. I couldn't pay for your schoolbooks. I couldn't do much of anything for any of you. It was very hard for me to accept that."

"But then you came home . . ."

"But then I came home and things were worse. I couldn't walk to the corner to buy a newspaper. I couldn't even get my clothes on without your mother's help. What good is a father who can't do anything for his children?"

I am crying, and I cannot help it. I sniffle and rub at my eyes to make them stop tearing.

"I missed you so much, Padar. I just wanted you to talk to us again. We all did."

"I missed you too, Obayda. And I want you to know that things will be different. Your uncle has been asking me to come work with him, and I think it's time. I have two capable hands I've been ignoring for too long."

A metal gate clangs and I wipe my eyes in a hurry. It's Agha Samir. He's headed our way with a five-gallon blue container. He's beaming from ear to ear as he walks toward us.

"Should we go, Padar?" My father hasn't socialized with the neighbors at all, and I wonder if he'd rather avoid a conversation. My father shakes his head and stays in the green chair. He picks up the walking stick he let drop and props it up against the chair's side arm. He straightens his back and pulls his shirt into place.

"Good morning!" Agha Samir hollers with a wave. "Well, well, I never imagined I'd be seeing my old school friend today. I'm glad I came out when I did. Brother, how have you been?"

"Samir." My father smiles. "It's good to see you, friend. It's been a lifetime, hasn't it?"

I watch Agha Samir's eyes float to my father's stump and stay there for a little too long before he collects himself and stops gawking.

"It sure has," Agha Samir agrees. "But when I think of it, it feels like yesterday. Do you remember all the trouble we used to get into? The time we used up all your mother's yarn to make kite strings?"

My father shakes his head with a soft laugh.

"She had just bought that yarn to make herself a sweater. She wouldn't speak to me for two days—thanks to you!"

"Me? You're the one who snuck the yarn out!"

"Yes, but I told her I hadn't touched it. She might've believed me if you hadn't blubbered out an apology."

I can't imagine my father lying to my grandmother.

"I couldn't help it." Agha Samir's belly rolls as he laughs deeply. "I felt so bad, I spent the next few weeks trying to learn how to knit so I could make it up to her, but the best I could do was a sock with no heel!"

I can't help but smile. Sometimes laughter is as contagious as a bad cold.

My father looks at me. I try to hide my grin, but the sparkle in his eyes tells me I don't need to.

"You haven't changed a bit," my father says, rubbing his neck.

"Not a bit?" he asks, rubbing his round belly. "I don't know if I'd agree with you on that, but I'm not one to argue with a long-lost friend. And you, you look . . . You look well."

Agha Samir fidgets and glances away as he says it.

"You're still a pathetic liar," my father says. He means it, but there's a little tease in his voice that tells Agha Samir he's already been forgiven for this fib.

Agha Samir rubs his forehead and shrugs.

"My fatal flaw," he admits with a sheepish smile.

Agha Samir's gaze drifts to me, with my curious boy hair and girl clothes. I'm sure he's thinking I look strange—like someone who is playing a bizarre dress-up game. I look at the ground and wish I could snap my fingers and make my boy clothes appear. Or even make my girl hair grow out instantly.

My father must feel the heat rising from my face. He takes the crutch and pushes himself to standing. Agha Samir rushes toward him, just as I did a few moments ago, but my father stops him with a raised hand. Agha Samir nods in understanding.

"I have all the help I need right here," he says slowly and confidently. He lifts the crutch a couple of inches off the ground and points at it with his eyes. "You see this stick? This has brought me back from the dead, nothing short of magic."

"It's a beauty," Agha Samir says. "Your brother must have made it for you."

"No," my father says with his eyes locked on Agha Samir's. I stand next to him and feel his fingers on my shoulder. "My brother's a good man, but this piece of magic is not his doing. My daughter made it for me. She's something special, my Obayda. She's my miracle."

Thirty-Three

With every step, my heart beats a little harder. I remember how nervous I was to go to school on my first day as a *bacha posh*. What was I thinking? That was nothing compared to what today is going to be like.

I asked my parents to let me stay home for a few more days, but they refused.

"It'll be fine," Meena tells me. I can feel her eyes on me even as I stare at the ground. I'm watching my girl feet inch their way down the road, and strange thoughts float through my head. If someone were to see my toes, would they mistake me for a boy? What about my hands or my ears? I know some parts of my body are definitely girl parts (I've been checking them pretty frequently to see if anything changed after my trip to the waterfall). But there are other parts of me that could go either way. My legs, the legs that climbed up the tree to get the perfect branch for my father's walking stick, are those girl legs or boy legs? And what about my brain?

"I can't believe I'm in a dress. This is such a horrible day."

"A horrible day?" Alia scoffs. "And you all say I'm the dramatic one!"

I know as soon as I say it that I am being whiny and unfair again, and I would hate for that to be my thing. I think back to the night my sisters stayed up with me when my parents decided to change me back into a girl. I bite my lower lip and try to look up a little. Meena wraps her arm around my shoulders.

I'm glad my head scarf is covering up my boy hair—or missing girl hair. I'm not sure what to call it yet.

As much as I drag my feet, there are only so many steps between our home and school. We are here and I see the boys kicking around a ball. Abdullah and Ashraf are in the middle of the group, but I spot them easily because they're taller than the others.

I take a step closer to Meena and try to disappear into her shadow. We're close enough that I'm breathing in the dust of their early morning soccer game. I pull the corner of my head scarf over my mouth and nose, not because of the dust but because I don't want to be recognized.

The girls are standing outside the school building in loose clusters. My sisters stay with me until it is time for us all to line up and step inside. The doors open and a teacher comes out to ring the bell. My eyes fall back on my shoes as the girls gather around us and form two lines. We enter the building, with me trying to be undetectable.

I follow Alia into her classroom. We're close enough in age that we are in the same class. I'm really grateful that I can be with her. She makes room for me next to her on the floor, but before I can sit down the teacher puts a hand on my shoulder.

"And you are?"

"Good morning, teacher. My name is . . . Obayda."

I wonder when my name will be my own again. Alia stands up.

"She's my sister, *Moallim-sahib*. She's with me."

"Ah, yes." The teacher looks at me and nods, like something's just occurred to her. "Obayda. Welcome to the class. I'm sure you'll settle in fine."

And then she does what I've been fearing she might do all night and with each step of my walk to school this morning.

"Class, please welcome Obayda. She is Alia's sister and was in one of the classes down the hall until a few days ago. Obayda, please stand up so everyone can meet you."

I want to say that I can't believe she's done this to me, but actually it's not surprising at all. Do all adults forget what it's like to be a kid?

I feel my face go from pink to white to red. My stomach turns upside down as twenty-five pairs of eyes turn to me. That's fifty eyes in total looking at a boy in girls' clothing. I slide back down to the floor as quickly as possible and the whispers start.

The *moallim* goes over a math lesson, and I try hard to pay attention, but I can't. I'm straining to hear every hushed voice behind me. I watch the back of every girl who fidgets in her place and wonder if she's itching to turn around and get a better look at the freak sitting behind her.

Alia looks over at me a few times and gives me sweet, reassuring smiles. That helps some, but there seem to be more and more whispers around me, and that's the only multiplication I can focus on.

When recess comes, I am so relieved. I plan to disappear into some hidden corner of the schoolyard. I remember the day Rahima chased me down and the way I retreated back into the building to get away from her. I wish she were here today so we could be girls together.

There's a lot of jostling to get out the door, though I know from experience that there's much more on the boys' side. I am shoulder to shoulder with Alia as we walk outside. I shield my eyes from the sun and start walking toward the side of the school most of the kids avoid.

"Where are you going, Obayda?" Alia asks.

"I just want to get away from everyone," I mumble. "You don't have to come with me. I know you have friends you usually play with."

"I'll stay with you," my sister says firmly. "I won't leave you alone."

"Hey, you!"

Alia begins to turn, but I tug at her elbow.

"Let's just keep moving."

"Alia!"

"What did she say her name was? Obayda!"

"Yeah, that's it. Obayda! We want to talk to you."

I can feel their eyes on my back. I steal a quick glance over my shoulder. I am expecting to see two or three girls. My stomach drops. There are at least sixteen girls by my quick count.

"Get back here! We know what you were!"

"It's not a secret! We all know!"

I squeeze my sister's arm so hard she grimaces. If it weren't for the mob of dresses behind us, she might have hit me. I can see she's as nervous as I am. What do they want from me? Are they going to tear off my head scarf? Are they going to circle around me and poke at me to figure out what I am now?

"Hurry, Alia!" I break into a jog. There are a few trees at the end of the schoolyard and then a small road. I know the school day isn't over, but I want nothing more than to run, run, run, as far as possible.

"Obayda, where are we going?"

"Home! I just want to go home!" When I hear my own voice shouting, I realize I'm crying, and that makes me so angry. What good is it to cry now? It's a sign of weakness, and I can't afford to look weak with a gang of feisty schoolgirls closing in on me.

I wipe my eyes with the back of my hand, but that makes everything even blurrier.

It's easy to run in pants, especially when surrounded by friends and laughing. Running in a skirt while crying and being chased by an angry mob—that doesn't work as well. My foot catches on a rock that I will hate for the rest of my life, and I stumble to the ground.

When I look up, the sun has disappeared. But it's not really gone. It's blocked by the heads of sixteen looming schoolgirls.

Thirty-Four

"**G**et away from me!" I yell and swing my arm in an arc. I wonder where Alia is. The girls have formed a tight circle around me and I feel completely trapped.

"Why are you running? We just want to talk to you."

I get on my feet and spin around, looking for an opening. The circle takes a collective step outward, widening enough for me to see Alia standing just behind another girl. She looks like she's trying to shoulder her way toward me.

"I'm running because you're chasing me! Why are you chasing me?"

One girl with a red barrette holding her head scarf in place puts both her hands on her hips and lets out a huff.

"We weren't *chasing* you. We wanted to talk to you. You're the one who started running."

My breathing slows. My eyes focus.

The girls around me are staring at me, but not in a scary way. They almost look like they've stumbled upon something dangerously exciting, like a forbidden movie, and are trying to see how close they can get without risking serious trouble.

"Why do you want to talk to me?"

The girl with the red barrette leans in. She seems to be the spokesperson of the group.

"We know what you were," she says softly.

I do a quick scan of the circle. All the girls are wide-eyed and motionless, as if someone pressed pause on their video player. I get a strange feeling in my chest and wait for her to go on. I'm still not sure what they want to do to me.

"Tell us."

"Tell . . . tell you what?" I stutter. Then I put my hands on my hips too, so that I match her pose. I need to not look like an easy target. "I'm not telling you anything!"

"Come on, you have to tell us!" pleads a girl with pistachio-colored eyes.

Alia pops out between two girls and takes a stand in the center of the circle along with me.

"She's got nothing to tell you! Leave my sister alone!"

she shouts, then drops her voice to a gravelly warning. "Or you'll be very, very sorry."

The circle widens a bit as everyone takes a half step back. They're a little unnerved by Alia's theatrical voice but not completely scared off. I'm glad my sister's here, but I also don't want her to defend me. I can't help but think of Rahima when I'm on this playground. She would never let herself feel cornered by a gang of girls.

"Now get away! All of you!" I yell and wave my arms around to shoo them off.

The circle of heads turn left and right, looking at one another for a cue. They shake their heads and the girl with pistachio eyes looks at me, confused.

"Why do you want to be so terrible to us? If I'd been a *bacha posh* like you, I'd be happy to talk about it. I'd want all the girls to know what it's like. Alia, you were wondering along with us just a few days ago."

Alia's brows furrow. "Is that what you want with Obayda?"

"Yeah, what was it like?"

"It must be so much better, isn't it?"

"Did you have to do any chores at home?"

"I think I could play soccer better than those boys. One of them always trips over the ball instead of kicking it. He's useless."

In a flash, I understand why they chased me.

I feel a long breath leave my body and realize I'd been holding it tight in my chest.

They don't want to do anything *to* me. They want to know what it was like to be a *bacha posh*, and I should not be surprised at all. I've seen them standing around while the boys knock knees over a soccer ball or cheer one another on in a game of *ghursai*. They watch out of the corners of their eyes, keeping a safe distance and never daring to play themselves because there are some things that girls just don't do. There are, actually, lots of things that girls don't do, but it's not because they don't want to.

"Being a *bacha posh* was the best thing that could've happened to me," I begin. Alia's shoulders relax, and she looks relieved that she doesn't have to stand up to the circle around us anymore. What I say next is not planned, but it comes out just right because it's how I honestly feel. "It's like when it's been freezing cold all winter and then— one day—it's suddenly spring and warm enough that you don't need a coat."

Sixteen pairs of eyes look like they're about to pop out of their heads. Everything they've been suspecting has just been confirmed, and I see the anger rising in them.

"I never had to go home straight after school. I didn't do any of the chores around the house. Everyone expected me to be loud, and it was fine if I went home with dirt on my pants. Nobody in the market cared where I was going, and I could climb trees without worrying about someone seeing my underpants."

Some girls are fuming. Others look skeptical. The girl with the red barrette looks like she's got a thousand more questions for me.

"Did you want to stay a *bacha posh*?"

"Of course I did! Why would I want to be a girl? What can you do in these . . . these . . . dresses?" I pull at my skirt and let it fall. Pants are made for legs, and legs are freedom. My father knows that just as well as I do.

"So you climbed trees and no one yelled at you?"

I shake my head.

"I climbed one of the tallest trees in the market. I even went up to the mountains—all by myself. You know, there are lots of snakes and scorpions on the mountains, and I saw some. Even had a scorpion walk across my foot, but it was too scared to sting me. I did lots of stuff that I can't even tell anyone about because it was so dangerous. I could do it because I was a boy."

The circle around me is buzzing with excitement. I'm trying not to gloat that I've made them all jealous with my experience, but how can I not, when I think about my adventures with Rahima, my games with Abdullah and Ashraf, the way I tricked the warlord's guards, and the crutch I made that got my father out of the house?

The smallest girl in the class steps forward. She's no

more than five inches from my face and much shorter than me.

"So you could do everything a boy could do?" she asks with a hint of mischief.

"Everything," I reply with confidence. I draw the word out and raise my eyebrows for effect. I wait for this little girl to be cowed by my cockiness, but she isn't—not in the least.

Instead, she tilts her head to the side and asks, in a voice that is sweet and venomous all at once: "If you could do everything a boy could do, could you pee standing up?"

Thirty-Five

It takes a few days, but I settle into life as a girl again. Things are different at home. I'm not the special son of the house anymore, but my father's also not wasting away in his room. He's been walking outside every day, and the color is back in his cheeks. We eat our meals together in the everything room. They're not the meaty dinners we used to have in Kabul, but somehow that doesn't matter when I look around and see the quiet smiles on my sisters' faces.

I'm thinking about this as I wander out of the classroom for recess. Alia's up ahead of me. She doesn't feel the need to stay by my side anymore. Since that day on the playground, my classmates are less intrigued by me. I can't blame them. All the cool stuff I did as a boy is history. And these girls are too old to even dream of being *bacha poshes*. I suppose sometimes people just have to accept what they are.

That's what I'm trying to do. I don't want to forget my adventures as Obayd, but I am also trying to be okay with being Obayda. I wear my Wizards cap only when I'm sleeping, but I do keep it in my schoolbag and tote it around every day—partly because I want to be able to give it back to Rahima if she ever shows up and partly because I wonder if it can still bring me good luck.

The boys on the other side of the yard are splitting off into two teams. Three boys are laying down rocks on opposite ends of the field. They're getting ready for a game of *ghursai*. Just watching them, my fingers and legs start to tingle. I wouldn't mind jumping in on their game.

"I can't believe you played *ghursai* with them," Pari says. She's the girl with the pistachio eyes.

"I know. It looks pretty tough. How do they hang on to their feet like that? I'd fall over in a second." Rabia is the girl with the red barrette. She's bold and would have been perfect as a *bacha posh*, I think. I haven't told her that I think so, but I probably should. I think she'd take it as a compliment.

"It's actually not as hard as it looks," I admit. "It was

tough at first and I fell down a lot, but after a few games I got the hang of it."

I turn my head so I'm not staring at the game. I don't want to make eye contact with Abdullah or Ashraf. I haven't spoken to them since I came back to school as Obayda, and I don't really want to. It couldn't be weirder if I'd grown a third arm.

"But you were a boy then. Maybe that's why you could do it," Pari suggests.

I wince at her comment.

"You know, I bet I could still do it. Actually, I bet you both could do it too."

Pari and Rabia break into wide grins.

"You think so?" Pari asks gently. "I don't know if that's such a good idea, since the teachers usually watch us from the classroom window and all . . ."

"Pari's probably right," Rabia says, but I can see a rebellious twinkle in her eyes.

I feel something electric run through me. I know how to make this work.

"That's fine. Maybe I can round up some of the other girls and—"

"No, I'll do it!" blurts Rabia.

"Me too," shouts Pari with a half-contained smile.

I put both hands on my hips and take a deep breath.

"Okay, so here's how it goes."

I bring them over to a mulberry tree since we'll need something they can balance on until they get the hang of it. I show them how to grab the toes of the opposite foot with their fingers and how to angle the wrist to get the best grip. Pari and Rabia stand next to the tree and whenever they start to wobble, they put a palm on the thick trunk and steady themselves. Pari manages to stand for a few seconds with one leg and one arm, so I tell her to try a hop or two. She does, and Rabia and I start to hoot and cheer. Pari's eyes get wide as if she can't believe her own feet. She turns to look at us, which throws her balance off completely and she lands on her bottom, the skirt of her dress flared out around her like a colorful mushroom.

"That was so good!" Rabia shouts. "My turn now."

Rabia manages to make a few hops, but she's teetering so much, any opponent would be able to knock her down.

"Don't look down," I coach. "Keep your eyes in the direction you want to go and don't stop moving. Your back has to stay straight or you'll have a harder time holding your grip on your feet."

Pari has gone around the tree and is giving Rabia a one-legged chase.

"I'm going to knock you down!"

Rabia laughs at the thought of Pari toppling her, but it's very possible. Pari's a natural.

And then I notice something. For the second time this

week, I'm in the center of a wide circle of gawking girls. This time, though, I'm sharing the attention with Pari and Rabia. Our classmates have gathered around us with nervous curiosity. Their eyes glisten with the same quiet rebellion, and that's all I need.

Rahima, I wish you could see this.

"You can all try it. It's not as hard as it looks."

"Oh, yes, it is!" yells Pari as she topples a couple of girls when she overshoots her hop. They laugh and push her back to standing. She beams at them before heading in a different direction. "Thanks!"

It starts with two girls. Then one more. Then three more. Before I can count, our half of the schoolyard is a field of one-legged girls. They are leaping, falling, and cheering each other on. We look like minnows out of water, flopping around ungracefully and totally out of our nature. But I watch them, and after a few moments the hopping takes on a rhythm. There are more girls standing than fallen. They are moving in a direction and squaring off against one another. They are *ghursai* players, ready for a match.

My eyes move from the sight of the girls to the boys, who have stopped their play to watch what they have never seen. Amidst the boys stand Ashraf and Abdullah. They must feel my gaze on them, because they turn in my direction and—before I can hide my face—our eyes meet.

They nod and jut their chins toward me in an expression that says they are impressed. I return their easy smiles. The communication between us is as clear as if I'd been standing at their side.

I can see, because I know them well enough, that they wish Rahima were here to see this too.

Thirty-Six

A lia runs up ahead of us. Her sandals kick up high behind her, and the hem of her skirt ruffles with her momentum. If she had pants on, she would be uncatchable—fast as any boy in our village.

"I can't wait to see it!" she calls out. Her voice carries back to us in the breeze. "Are you sure we'll be able to find it?"

"Not with you leading the way," I tease.

I shake my head. It's starting to get warm enough that running isn't such a great idea. She'll be thirsty for water soon, and we've got a ways to walk still. I should know.

Neela and Meena walk in front of me.

I turn to look back at my mother. She's standing by the metal gate of our home with my baby brother in her arms. His head rests against the dip between her shoulder and neck, and she's lifted his cotton shirt so his back can absorb some early morning light. My mother says the sunlight is good for him. Even from a few yards away, I can see his tiny eyes squint against the brightness, which will lull him to sleep.

My baby brother's golden-brown hair catches the sun. In the week before he joined us, we debated whether he would look like my mother or my father. No one expected, when he was born, that he would share my caramel-brown eyes, my dimpled chin, and my tapered fingers. When he yawns, his miniature nose wrinkles up just like mine does. Even I am surprised. He is the boy version of me, and because of that I can't help but love him just a little more than I would otherwise.

My mother waves at us once more before we are completely out of sight. She goes back into the house, where she'll spend the rest of the morning preparing a hearty dinner. She knows we'll come back hungry. My father walks next to me. His walking stick is at his side, as it always is. The padding's gotten pretty worn, but I'm proud of that. It's worn through because he's been using it so much. I've got ideas on how to make a better cushion to replace this one soon.

"Remember, watch your step. There are scorpions around—"

"And snakes," I add.

My father looks at me with eyebrows raised. "The more advice you give us, the more I shake to think of you having done this alone."

I look at the ground to hide my grin. It is pretty amazing that I've already made this trip once and that I did it on my own.

Neela is carrying a bag with a few snacks. She packed them this morning expecting that Alia and I would be asking for something soon. She's always ready for anything, I think as I watch her back. And she's strong enough that, if she really needs to, she could carry Alia or me. Watching her steady stride, I can't help but think Neela would have been a great *bacha posh*.

This trip was Meena's idea. When she proposed it, my mother shook her head and rejected it immediately. I don't blame her. I'm sure she was thinking of what I looked like when I finally came home after my trek to the mountains. It's hard to forget the scrapes on my hands, the blisters on my feet, and my clothes wet with mountain water. But Meena doesn't let anything go, and once that idea popped into her head it wasn't going anywhere until she saw the waterfall with her own eyes.

Come to think of it, Meena would have been a really good *bacha posh* too.

"Padar?"

"Yes, Obayda?"

"I'm really glad you're bringing us out here." There's a lot buried in my statement. Here's what I don't say because my throat would close up with emotion if I tried: *I'm proud of how hard you've worked to get stronger. And I'm so glad to have you around as our father again. And I know you don't wish that we were anything but your daughters.* My father blinks twice and his lips tighten, which tells me he understands all that I didn't come right out and say.

"I'm really glad I can do this too. I can't believe I'm bringing my girls to a place I used to go to as a boy. Everything's changed so much for us since we left Kabul."

I nod in agreement. It seems like a lifetime ago that my father had two legs, when it's only been about a year. Lots has happened in that time. I went from being Obayda to Obayd and back to Obayda. I had no friends, then I had Rahim, and now I have the memories of Rahima and lots of new friends like Pari and Rabia. I'm not the special child in the house anymore, but I'm okay with that. I like being one of the sisters, and I'm pretty sure my little brother is going to be in good hands with all of us looking after him. We've got lots to teach him. And in this year I've realized that I have a thing too—I'm the girl that can do some really surprising stuff.

We are in the open field now, and I can see the mountains ahead. I see the camel with her earthy humps and head resting on the horizon.

I know I've been told that the myth about passing under a rainbow changing girls to boys is nothing but superstition. Still, a small part of me thinks that ever since I clung to those rocks for dear life and let the waterfall cascade over me, something has changed.

A gentle breeze sweeps down from the east, putting a lift in our step. It rushes ahead of my family and me, as if to lead the way. In the distance, I can almost see the gust race up the mountain, circle around the camel's neck, and drift down to the cluster of tall grasses that I imagine to be the camel's flirtatious eyelashes. Tickled by the wind, the grasses bend and rise, and I can't help but laugh at the mountain camel's wink, as if she and I will always share a secret.

Author's Note

I was raised by parents who never clipped my wings. They taught me by example that girls and boys are equal in what they can achieve. I was cocooned with an extended family who applauded achievements and encouraged aspirations others might have reserved only for boys. For that, I am eternally grateful, for I would be a different person if I'd been taught that I should expect anything less from myself.

Though this story is set in Afghanistan, my hope is that it will inspire dialogue and reflection about the meaning of gender in any land. I chose Afghanistan as the setting because it is the homeland of my family, and also because, when it comes to gender inequality, Afghanistan is infamous.

It wasn't always this way, but the years of war and rise of brutally misogynistic regimes including the Taliban shuttered women in their homes and reduced them to shadows. From such a plummeting fall, there was nowhere to go but up. In a swift and steep effort to recover lost ground, Afghan girls and women are bravely stepping into the sun. Who are today's Afghan women? They are fist-pumping politicians, soaring pilots, determined pupils, poised newscasters, bold artists, savvy businesswomen, probing journalists, and more.

And what about the *bacha posh*?

The longstanding *bacha posh* tradition of Afghanistan is a curiosity for many, but it is also a remarkable way to explore what it means to be a girl. Families without a son may designate a young daughter to fill that void with a simple physical transformation involving swapping out clothing and cutting hair. Before she reaches puberty, the *bacha posh* (girl dressed as a boy) is changed back and resumes life as a girl, a gender that enjoys far less liberty and privilege.

The *bacha posh* tradition exists because sons are valued in a way daughters are not. It exists because there is a perception that boys are capable of things girls are not. Are these thoughts unique to Afghanistan? Sadly, not at all.

There are many ways to devalue girls. It can be as flagrant as barring girls from school or forcing them to become brides when they should be learning to read. It can also be as insidious as jeering that someone "throws like a girl" or not blinking when a girl's voice is interrupted by that of a boy.

The *bacha posh* is a powerful teacher. By a simple change in attire, her potential changes. Her confidence is lifted. Her worth is multiplied. And yet, she is the same person underneath the shallow veneer of boyhood.

The moment we see past gender and look at the heart of a child, we will see a world of potential that can take him or her all the way to the mountaintop. What a world it would be to see them all soar under the warmth of a proud and nurturing sun.

A Note About Pronunciation

What's in a name? In Afghanistan, there is great importance placed on the meaning of names. Obayda (Oh-BUY-dah) is a name derived from the Arabic language and means "one who is faithful or loyal." Oftentimes, the male version, Obayd (Oh-BUYD), may be extended as Obayd-allah, meaning one who is faithful to God (Allah).

Acknowledgments

If it takes a village to raise a child, then books and children have something in common.

My thanks to Helen Heller for believing Rahima should reach a younger audience and for, yet again, gracing the story with Rumi's wisdom. My gratitude to Sarah Heller for your astute guidance, and for placing the manuscript in the nurturing hands of Rosemary Brosnan. Rosemary, you and your formidable team have humbled me with the enthusiasm you have for putting Obayda's tale in the hands of the most important readers—children.

To those closest to me, thank you for the support, the confidence, the inspiration, the critique, and, sometimes, the material. Amin, Mom, Dad, Zoran, Zayla, Kyrus, and Cyra—you are my reasons for writing.

Don't miss the next heartfelt
and adventurous story
from Nadia Hashimi . . .

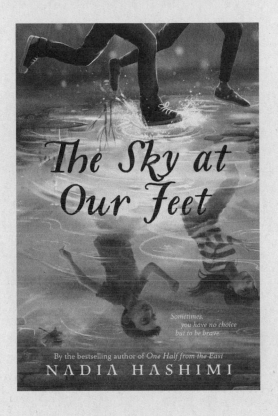

Turn the page for a sneak peek at *The Sky at Our Feet*!

One

Pigeons, no matter what country they live in, share a few important traits. They are smart birds that can learn aerial tricks and navigate their way back home. They will eat just about anything. Carrots, lettuce, bell peppers, rice, and crumbled-up bread. They're not very picky. They do need grit to digest their food, though. That could be little pieces of gravel or ground-up oyster shells if you happen to have oyster shells around.

I do not. There aren't many oysters in this overcrowded city in New Jersey. I can't imagine that there are many oyster shells in Afghanistan either, since the country doesn't touch the ocean.

But there's plenty of gravel around thanks to the

crumbling cement of the chimney and building trim, so the birds on our roof are doing okay. I put out fresh bowls of water for them. I change the water every couple of days. Sometimes the rain does the work for me.

I look up. An airplane has left a thin trail of white cotton behind it. Since I was little, my mother has tested me with riddles she learned as a child in Afghanistan. Each one is a mystery, and I like the challenge of unlocking them. I close my eyes and remember one of them.

What searches the skies without ever leaving its home?

I figured out the answer to that one quicker than she expected.

An eye, I remember saying.

I'm not really supposed to be up here on the roof. My mother wouldn't be too happy if she knew I came up here almost every day to try to train pigeons. Our building is old, and the roof sags in some parts. There isn't any kind of railing either, so I have to be sure I stay clear of the edges. But it's safe if you know what you're doing, and I've been doing this for about a year, after my mom told me about what some of her neighbors used to do back in Afghanistan, long before she moved to New Jersey.

"Leave him alone," I mutter. Of the nine pigeons that live on our roof, Billy is the worst. He's always shoving his way to the food as if he's got more right to it than anyone else. There's nothing that special about him, but he seems to think there is. There's one that's more tan than gray. He (or she) might be older than the others. He's got a scar on one side of his face and doesn't move as fast. The others are pretty timid. It took a long time for them not to fly off the rooftop as soon as I opened the hatch to climb up here. Now they gather around because they know I'll bring something good for them.

They fly off but always come back. I haven't gotten them to do any tricks like the pigeon trainers in Afghanistan have done, but I'm working on it. My mom told me her neighbor back home had pigeons who could do full loops or fly with their bellies up. They would fly miles away to deliver secret messages tied to their feet but still come back home. My pigeons are nowhere close to doing any of that, but if lots of other Afghans have been able to do it, I think there's got to be a way.

I'm about to toss out chunks of buttered bread when a voice catches me off guard.

"What are you doing here?"

I drop the plastic bag I'm holding and spin around. Ms. Raz, our landlord and first-floor neighbor, has poked her head out of the hatch.

"I was just—"

But Ms. Raz is not your average silver-haired woman. She doesn't knit or watch game shows or moan about her aching back. I never see or hear her coming, and yet there she always is, suspicious and cranky.

"Get off the roof this minute! You're not supposed to be up here."

Neither is she, really, unless she wants to have her other hip replaced.

"Sorry," I mumble, trying to hide the bowl of water and rice from Ms. Raz's squinty glare.

Ms. Raz is waiting for me when I climb down the ladder and go back into the building. She follows me as I walk, shoulders slumped, to our third-floor apartment. Each floor is one apartment with windows overlooking the street or the grocery store parking lot behind us. The roof is the only place that gives a view of Elkton. I can see the roof of my school to the east and the train station to the south. I see the road that leads to the laundromat and the park where I broke my arm on the monkey bars.

My mother is inside our top-floor apartment, about to be sorely disappointed by what I've just been caught doing.

"Ms. Raz," I say, trying to find a way out of this. It's October and winter is only a couple of months away. Maybe I could offer to shovel the snow off the sidewalk and steps again.

"Not a chance. Open that door so I can tell your mother where I found you." Ms. Raz's glasses hang on a thin chain around her neck. She's looking at me, waiting for my move. The floorboards creak as I shift my weight and stall.

"Shah-jan, is that you?" my mother's voice calls out from inside the apartment. "Come so we can cut this beautiful cake!"

The cake. This gives me an idea. It'll only work if there's a warm heart somewhere inside Ms. Raz's chest.

"She's been waiting for me," I explain. "It's her birthday today, and I saved some money and bought her a chocolate cake. Would you like a slice?"

Ms. Raz folds her arms across her chest and huffs something about bringing her plants in from the balcony.

"If I ever catch you up there again, I'll have you out of this building in a heartbeat!"

I nod my head solemnly and wait for Ms. Raz to disappear before I open the door. I don't want my mother to spot her standing behind me and figure out I took a detour on my way to pick up the mail.

"*Salaam*, Madar!" I call out. My mother is in the small kitchen with her back turned toward me. I can see her light-blue jeans, her ponytail frizzy from the humidity of the laundromat where she works. The evening news plays in the background. My mom always has the news on, as if there's something she's waiting to hear.

I never really learned much Dari from my mother, but

she does insist that I greet her as all Afghans do, so I say *salaam*, which means peace.

"*Salaam, jan-em!*" she sings. She spins to face me, and I see a plate of seasoned drumsticks and stewed potatoes on our little kitchen table. There's the tiny cake I bought too, with one skinny candle sticking out of it. "I make your favorite foods!"

My mom always wants to practice her English with me, so all our conversations are in English. It's my job to correct her pronunciation and grammar, though she's not always happy when I do it.

"It's your birthday, though, so you should have *made* your favorite foods," I correct her without thinking. The cake is actually a cupcake, but it's all I could afford. It's covered with sprinkles and it takes a lot of self-control not to dip my finger into it for a taste. I'm grateful this moment hasn't been ruined by Ms. Raz.

"How was your school today?" she says, ignoring my correction. She kisses the top of my head and points me to the sink so I can wash my hands.

"Fine," I say. I turn the handle and water sputters out. I give the handle an extra twist and it comes off in my hand. It's an old building, so something's always cracking, leaking, shaking, or breaking. My mom and I have become pretty good at fixing most of it ourselves so we don't have to bother Ms. Raz too often. I open the cabinet under the sink and turn off the water valve so the water won't spray everywhere. Then I reach into our tool drawer and pull a wrench from the pile of dollar-store tools. I twist the tip of the faucet off and find a mesh piece inside. I scrub off some gunk and put the pieces back together. "How was work?"

My mother is standing in front of the television, listening to the news anchor. He's talking about a rally against people who are in this country illegally. I see a picture of people shouting and waving signs around. The signs say things like *America for Americans* and *Go Home*.

I slip the small rubber ring off the inside of the handle. It's torn and there's no way to fix it. I dig into the tool drawer again and find a rubber band. I wrap it around the inside of the handle twice and slide it into place. I put the pieces back together and re-open the valve beneath the sink.

"Ha!" I say, happy to see the rubber band did the trick.

"Dear God," my mother says in Dari.

"What's the matter, Mom?" I say, drying my hands on a rag. I follow her gaze to the television screen and see the angry protest, the things they're saying about people who snuck into the country. "They're just mad at people who broke the rules. You get just as mad when I break rules. Remember what you did when I watched an extra half hour of television last Tuesday?"

I laugh at my own joke.

My mother does not.

"Mom, are you okay?"

She looks like she might cry. She also looks like there's something she wants to tell me. As a matter of fact, she's looked that way for the past few weeks. I suppose I've been waiting for this moment, though I didn't know exactly what I was waiting for.

"Shah-jan," she says slowly. "Me and them—we are the same."

What can she possibly mean by that? She's got nothing in common with those people. My mother doesn't speak Spanish. She didn't sneak into this country in the middle of the night. She speaks English and works a regular job.

"Sit down. It is time I tell you my story."

Suddenly my stomach is on edge. I am nervous. I've asked my mom a million times to tell me stories about Afghanistan. Sometimes she describes a place that sounds like heaven.

The fruits taste like they've been sprinkled with sugar. People open their homes even to strangers so travelers are always fed and cared for. The mountains are tall and proud, more impressive than any skyscraper. Every home has a poet and every home has a musician because words and music give Afghans life. Afghanistan is home to the best horsemen—they can defy gravity on the back of a stallion.

For honor and family, an Afghan will go to the ends of the earth. Celebrations are rich and festive—a time for new clothes and money handed to smiling children.

Other times, she winces and just changes the subject. I think that's when she's remembering the not-so-great stuff about Afghanistan. I have a feeling she's going to tell me about that stuff now, and I don't know if I want to hear it.

I sit down at the table. My mother joins me.

"Some things I never told you. But maybe I tell you now why I cannot go back. When I see this," she says, pointing to the angry faces on the television screen, "I don't know what is possible to happen." She leaves the television on. My eyes float between looking at my mother and looking at the protestors.

I don't know how, but I have a feeling that, unlike our leaking faucet, the problem my mother's about to reveal has no quick fix.

Great books by
NADIA HASHIMI!

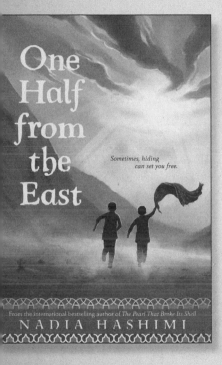

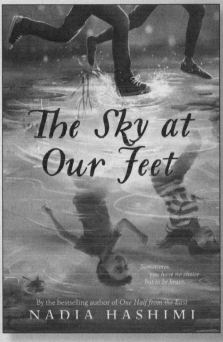